Paper Kisses

N.J. Lysk
Uncommon Paths, book 2.

Copyright

Summary

An alpha werewolf. A human. A whole week of St. Valentine's celebrations.

Abel's life hasn't gone according to plan. When he was just out of school, he found an omega he loved and they had a child together. Now that omega just got mated to someone else. He is determined to enjoy more time with their daughter and be happy for his ex, but he still has too much time on his hands, so when Eve's school organizes a whole week of St. Valentine's celebrations, he confronts the teacher in charge.

If there's one thing Deryn knew he wanted, it was teaching, but the actual work requires long hours and a lot of thinking on his feet. Plus, in his small Welsh hometown, there isn't much socializing for a gay man that wants more than a quickly forgotten anonymous encounter.

Meeting the man of his dreams in his very classroom seems too lucky to be true, so naturally it turns out Abel is the parent of one of his students.

"Paper Kisses" is a sweet M/M Age Gap Romance.

Thank you to **AJ Bixler**, **Gema Cela Rodríguez** and **Elouise East** for beta reading, sensitivity check and this impossible title!

Chapter 1

ABEL

The thing was, he wasn't actually made of stone.

It was hard to see Tristan blooming like that under the worshipful light of his new alpha's attention. But it wasn't an *alpha* thing. It was completely normal to feel sad when your first and only love found someone else, wasn't it? He wasn't angry with either Tristan or Lyall, just plain old jealous.

At least he was fairly sure they were too caught up in each other to notice.

And he was busy with Eve, since his daughter had asked to spend more nights at his place now that her dad had something other than work to keep him busy.

"They are just so..." She told him that night at dinner, a moue of disgust twisting her pretty face that had nothing to do with Abel's slow-cooked stew.

"Sappy?" he offered sympathetically, taking a bite of bread.

Eve sighed, dipping her spoon in her bowl but not bringing the food to her mouth. "Yeah, and, like, it's *all* the time. Even when they're working!"

"I'm sure your dad isn't being unprofessional," Abel argued.

"No, it's not—" She huffed, taking a chug of her Ribena, a preference no werewolf could justify. "I can just *feel* it, and Lyall is always *looking* at dad."

"Looking sounds awful," he teased, smirking when his daughter rolled her eyes at him with all the promise of her upcoming teenagehood. She was going... Hell, she was *already* a handful. And he couldn't have been happier to have her around more.

"You don't know how bad it gets," she declared.

"Well, pup, guess you'll have to be good here so I don't send you back," he told her, spooning some broccoli onto her plate.

"Ugh, daddy, don't call me that!" she moaned, eyeing the vegetables in despair but knowing not to argue. "What if a human hears you?"

He didn't point out there were no humans in their kitchen, shrugging instead. "They would think I'm eccentric."

"They would think you are a *weirdo*," she corrected, stabbing the tiny trees with gusto.

St. Valentine's *Week* was just the last straw.

"A week?" he repeated when Eve told him.

She shrugged. "It's love around *the world*, it takes time to prepare."

"And this is supposed to help you learn Spanish and French?"

"No," she told him sternly. "It's supposed to teach me about different cultures."

"Then why St. Valentine's? Pretty sure they don't do that in... Thailand or whatever."

"Ugh, *dad*," Eve huffed, yanking her books out of her school bag. "It's just a name!"

He must have been really crossing a line if Eve was calling him 'dad'. He'd always been 'daddy', earning the title by virtue of being around when she'd started speaking while Tristan was away at university for most of the week.

"Okay, okay," he said, hands up and palms out.

She kept a suspicious eye on him, then went back to spreading her tools all over the living room table.

There were at least a dozen envelopes of glitter—Abel's place was going to be sparkling for a while, and possibly also his fur if he knew anything about glitter. Thank the Moon they no longer had to deal with hunters or they'd have ended up getting killed over sparkling in the dark.

Normally, Eve got back home on the bus, but he'd had to drive to the city centre to deliver a bookshelf for a client so he'd figured he could save her a trip.

So naturally it was the one day she had an afterschool club.

He told the receptionist he'd just wait and gingerly sat on one of the plastic chairs, not quite trusting it to support his weight. He didn't mean anything by it when he asked him who was in charge of the glaringly pink decorations covering the walls and ceiling.

"Oh, that would be Mr Deryn," the young guy told him cheerily. "He's still looking for volunteers, if you got time to kill..."

He was pretty informal for a receptionist, but then again, most people assumed Abel was in his early twenties—werewolves everywhere were subjected to getting asked for ID well into their forties. They could hardly complain about good health, so they had to put up with the shocked looks and suspicion. Once upon a time, suspicion from a human could have meant death, now it meant carrying your driver's license around.

He checked the time, then decided to go for it. Eve might complain about him embarrassing her in front of a teacher, but this was a teacher who thought spending a week on a stupidly commercial tradition was worth their time. And anyway, didn't they always say there were no stupid questions?

The door he'd been pointed towards was open, but even if it hadn't been, there was no missing the overwhelmingly pink and red decorations strewn about the place. "Hello?"

He could hear a heartbeat, but it took him a moment to locate its source.

The guy who looked up had thick dark eyelashes framing honey-coloured eyes. As close to wolf eyes as humans ever got and fitting with the rest of the pretty face.

Except for the dark circles under the man's eyes.

Abel cleared his throat, suddenly uncomfortable, but the state of the room only encouraged him. There were a pair of gigantic entwined hearts leaning against the back wall.

DERYN

"M̲r Deryn?" The deep voice broke him out of the reverie of prolonged cutting and gluing. The man leaning against his doorway was a lot closer to art than anything Deryn had come up with for the international celebration. Tall and solid, with long eyebrows and a thin nose that looked dignified with his high cheekbones.

He didn't manage to respond before the guy nodded and straightened to his full height. Deryn swallowed hard under the weight of his blue eyes. "Thing is... I hate to complain, but my kid's spent the last three days cutting out *paper hearts*."

Deryn blinked at him and managed to keep his voice even. Of course it had to be a parent. "So?"

The guy stepped inside. "So how is that teaching her anything?" And damn, the furrowed brow ruined the whole aristocratic look, but it didn't detract from how beautiful his features were.

"I'm sorry, Mister...?" Deryn put down the scissors, resigning himself to this conversation.

"Mathonwy."

It took a moment for the odd name to penetrate and then he remembered who it also belonged too. "You're Eve's... father." He glanced away, needing a second to recover. It wasn't every day he discovered one of his students had queer parents, but he'd met Eve's dad. Other dad, it seemed.

"Yes." The other man clearly noticed the hesitation and Deryn bit his tongue to keep back the urge to apologize, or worse, explain the surprise wasn't judgement.

He'd made a choice when he'd left Manchester after uni and returned home, and part of that choice meant he didn't have a community to support him. He could deal; he almost never had time to go out anywhere in any case. And most people who went to uni didn't come back to Criccieth.

"Did Eve mention that we voted on what the theme for the international week should be?" he asked, keeping his eyes in the vicinity of the other man's cheekbones.

"What? No." Mr Mathonwy took a step closer and took a seat in one of the few desks not covered by paper hearts. He was lucky Deryn had just hung them up by the doorway like a weirdly pink version of mistletoe—another silly tradition, but the kids would get a kick out of it and he had included the words for 'kiss' in every Romance language among the hearts.

"We did," he told Eve's father, trying for neutral. "Our class has more girls than boys, they voted St. Valentine's since it's February. I pointed out they didn't have it in most countries so... love it was."

Mathonwy's lips thinned. "Isn't that a bit sexist?"

Deryn stared, barely able to hold back a laugh.

"Yes," he agreed after a moment. "But given that we live in a culture that indoctrinates girls to think of romance as their highest goal, it's also not that surprising that most of them buy into it."

The blue eyes narrowed, but then the other man's face opened up. "Fair," he declared. "But shouldn't you try to, dunno, break them out of it?"

"Pretty sure that's above my pay grade," Deryn said, mostly amused. He did try, of course he tried, as much as he could without it becoming a crusade or something. He could be a safe place, but he didn't want to lose track of what he was actually supposed to do, namely, somehow get them all to the point where they could speak French or Spanish, in some incredibly rare cases both. "Possibly above yours too," he pointed out, not quite willing to take the lecture lying down.

He got a snort in response. "Oh, I'm good," Mathonwy assured him easily, a small smile dancing on his lips. "Eve's other dad won't shut up about this stuff."

"Yeah?" Deryn asked, trying for casual.

He thought the intense look he got in response meant he hadn't quite managed to disguise his interest. "Have you met Tristan? He's the one Eve gets her tan from," he added, the smile self-deprecating. Deryn smiled back. It was a quirky way to say his black partner was Eve's biological father.

He was also the one who got his surname first on her paperwork. Deryn had thought it was odd they hadn't gone for alphabetical order like most families. "Yes, but I didn't realise..."

"He's a doctor, researcher," Mathonwy clarified, eyes bright and obviously proud and, damn, Deryn wanted someone to look like that when they talked about *him*. "Anyway," said Mathonwy, offering a hand. "I'm Abel. Is Deryn a first or last name?"

He took the proffered hand but couldn't find words for a moment. "First," he said at last, squeezing quickly.

Abel's hand was hot in his, fingers rough against his palm as they let go. Deryn made himself offer a smile and meet his eyes. *Professional*, he reminded himself.

His guest glanced around. "Does everything need to be pink? Can love be a little more colourful or something?" he suggested.

Was he...? But Deryn could ask, of course. "Like a rainbow?" He was not quite able to hold back a smile, but what the hell, the guy had backed down and finding a man who didn't think being right was more important than anything else was rare enough that Deryn was happy to take advantage.

Strangely, the other man seemed surprised at the suggestion. "Sure! See? You *can* make things a little less sexist."

"What about you?" Deryn demanded, a tad annoyed. He'd thought they'd agreed to let it go.

Abel did a double-take, then laughed aloud, deep and true. "Yeah," he said, voice full of amusement. "I can make things. I'm a carpenter, I'm good with my hands."

Deryn exhaled, determined to thank him and tell him he didn't need the help, when Abel pointed at the corner. "That desk looks like it could use a hand."

"What?" He turned to see where he was pointing.

It was the desk that always creaked—the very one the most immature of his students enjoyed taking so they could rock their chair while holding on to it and irritate the ever-loving fuck out of Deryn.

He'd been stuck with it, of course, there wasn't money to buy a new one and it'd been in his classroom when he'd arrived. "That... okay," he said a little stiffly.

"Great!" Abel stood up. "I'll have a look at it first..." he said, glancing at Deryn for what he thought was permission.

Deryn waved him ahead, he didn't even like ordering children around. The point of a teacher was to guide someone to the path of learning, not drag them there, and Deryn was perfectly willing to admit when he wasn't an expert on a subject. "Please."

If anyone had asked him, he'd have guessed you needed special tools for carpentry, but Abel seemed just fine with a cutter from Deryn's desk and a screwdriver he'd either been carrying around or had found somewhere in the chaos of the room. He flipped the desk with the ease most people used to flip pillows. Deryn might have stared a little at his bare arms—when had he discarded his jacket and why was anyone wearing short sleeves in *February*?

He yanked his attention back to the poster he was laminating. He could use it again next year, he figured. He wasn't always going to have to do this much work, he just needed to create enough resources to make his classes interesting and then it'd get easier.

At least he hoped so.

ABEL

The desk was an easy enough fix once he loosened the screws and put them back in with a little glue and sawdust to make up the space where the wood had been eaten away by the continuous movements of the front leg.

He hoped it made up for his comments. He hadn't been trying to be judgemental, he was just... Well, bored as fuck. Eve was pretty much the only person he talked to on a regular basis lately and it seemed like she'd been getting busier and busier. And she was only thirteen, what would happen when she was a proper teenager?

He had his pack, of course, no wolf was ever truly alone. But his friends had all paired up, even the betas, and most of them had little kids. None of them had got their best friend pregnant at twenty. They were busy, with their families and work, and life.

There were pack meetings and luncheons on Sundays and Abel mostly attended, even if Eve and Tristan didn't. But it wasn't quite enough to make up for the rest of the week, for most his hours when there was no one to turn to and share a joke or a ridiculous story he'd caught on the radio.

He hadn't realised how much he'd relied on Tristan until his friend had found someone else. Tristan had always been around. It hadn't mattered that much that they weren't together—friendship and sex and companionship were more than enough for Abel.

But Tristan had Lyall now, and thanks to Lyall his work had doubled or maybe tripled—it was hard to keep track—and when he wasn't working, he was with Lyall himself.

Abel couldn't really complain about that, could he?

Supposedly, Eve should have been spending all that much more time with Abel as a consequence, but Eve wasn't a little kid, she'd do homework after school or go hang out with her friends either in a café or their homes. Never at his, he thought she didn't like to advertise the fact that her parents were not together. She came back on time for dinner every day, and sometimes she even asked for help with a poster or a diagram, but other than that, homework was not Abel's forte.

So he was left with this, complaining to a teacher about a silly party just so he could argue with someone about something that wasn't bedtime or schoolwork, or in his mother's case—why he was still single at thirty-three when there were so many nice omegas in their pack and the neighbouring ones.

He put the desk back on its legs, shaking it a little to check his work. It was fine.

Deryn didn't seem to notice, intent on cutting... yellow paper?

Abel cleared his throat. "Um, can I help with something else?"

Dark eyelashes blinked up at him. "Oh, is it fixed?"

"It could use a thicker screw," Abel offered. "But it's stable now."

It was the advantage of being able to use his strength to secure the screws as deep as they would go.

"You want to test it, Mr Deryn?" he asked, teasing when he saw the other man's eyes wander to it.

"No need," he was told. "I'm sure... Um, thank you," he finished, eyes meeting Abel's for just a moment. It made Abel wonder how he dealt with a rowdy classroom, he was a small guy and seemed a little skittish and kids could smell weakness like sharks could blood.

"You want me to do another colour?" Abel offered. The sheer amount of material on the desks was overwhelming, he couldn't imagine...

"You want to cut paper hearts?" Deryn shot him a look that made his disbelief clear. Maybe not so shy, after all.

Abel raised his hands. "Well, it was my idea to make them more colourful. It's not fair to give you even more work without offering to help out. But, say, aren't we wasting paper?"

Deryn actually groaned at that. "Are you an ecologist too? I don't think I can quite live up to your standards."

Abel grimaced. "Sorry, I just—"

He got interrupted by an eye roll. "I'm giving them to the supply teacher who's been handling the classroom next door. She doesn't stay late so the place won't have anything for International Week if I don't do it."

Abel nodded, a little relieved to be let off the hook. "Isn't that... I mean, are you the department head?"

Deryn snorted, looking down at himself like something about his curly dark hair or fine features should have made the notion absurd. "Me? No! I'm only twenty-four."

"Well," Abel said, smiling a little. He always had a hard time telling with humans, back when Tristan and he had been kids, the pack had home-schooled their children until secondary school. Apparently not seeing humans regularly messed up with your ability to read the marks of ageing as well as put you quite out of touch with popular culture. He still cringed to remember the first few weeks of year 7, though at least he'd had Tristan and Bina with him. "You are very dedicated, I'm sure you'll get far."

"Not sure department head is far," Deryn said with a cynicism that belied his age. "But thanks, I guess."

"So... purple?" Abel offered, cutter at the ready. No way could he get his fingers into those child-sized scissors.

"Um." Deryn's eyes were really something else, luminous and wide. "Second drawer," he indicated, and Abel went for it.

It was as good a way to pass half an hour as any other, and he was... curious. About this young human who could probably give Tristan a run for his money with the speeches but seemed resigned to things staying the same. It was... well, sad.

Abel wasn't out to change the world, not beyond making sure his pack was safe and happy and his pieces made to last. But then again, he hadn't taken a job as a teacher—probably underpaid if it required one to stay after hours to decorate the place.

"Glitter's in the left drawer of the desk," Eve's teacher told him, eyes intent on the tangled mess of coloured threads they were using to hang the hearts. Despite the banality of the task, he seemed lost in it. Abel was familiar with the sensation from his own work—creating something with his hands let him find a peace inside his head that normally only his wolf knew the way to.

A few hours working left him feeling like he'd put his thoughts in order instead of sanded some parts and carefully fitted them together.

He took the tubes of glitter to the table without complaint. In any case, Eve had spilled enough all over their sofa that a little more could only add to the discontinuous shimmer of his clothes.

"Do you like crafts?" he asked, twisting strands to create a paper basket—it was quite ingenious, really, even if the colour scheme was already giving him a headache. Who had decided love was pinks and reds? Or that it should be bright colours and sparkling arrangements?

But you could only make the baskets in two colours so the rainbow combination he'd used for the hearts hanging across the room wouldn't work. He couldn't stomach wasting the paper, anyway. Compared to wood, used to make objects that would last for years—if not decades—paper seemed like a serious waste of plant life.

"Mmm... yeah." Deryn's eyes were mostly honey but the specks of gold stood out all the more starkly for the contrast. Abel was an artist and he could not miss it, that was all. "Mainly sculpture."

"Oh, clay?" Abel asked. He'd done it in school and he'd really enjoyed it—if he hadn't been so fed up with writing essays, he might have gone on to study art instead of finding an apprenticeship.

"Paper."

"Paper?" he echoed, blankly.

The pretty eyes flickered away, but he could feel the other man's attention on him. "Yeah, you cut it up real tiny and stick it together, mostly with tweezers. It's quite amazing what some people do. It's a cheap hobby," he added, flashing Abel a smile that was probably meant to be self-deprecating.

It would have worked if Abel had resisted the impulse to stare at his lips.

He swallowed, reminding himself of how limited human senses were. Not that a wolf would have called him out on such a little thing. "You got some pictures?"

"Um, yeah..." Those golden eyes went back to the big desk—probably where his phone was—but then he shook his head. "I should really buy you a coffee after all this, though. There's a place around the corner..." The offer started out casual enough but the human's heartbeat picked up as the words tumbled out and he dipped his chin to hide his face.

"Oh, I—" Abel's wolf perked up, much more attuned to the subtle shifts in a person's body language. Then his human brain reminded him of a little fact. "Chess," he said with true regret. "Eve should be done by now... But next time?"

DERYN

"**Y**ou can owe me," Abel said, startling him into looking up. "Pay up when I come back to fix that desk."

Deryn slanted a look at the furniture in question. "I thought it was fixed already."

"It won't last, not without a thicker screw."

"Oh."

"It's perfectly safe," Abel insisted, like he assumed health and safety regulations were the cause of Deryn's silence.

"Sure, thank you. I... You should go get Eve," he said, trying to be gently encouraging and not sound like he wanted the nice man who'd been helping him out for the heck of it to go away as soon as possible.

Embarrassment was no justification for rudeness.

The weird thing was that Abel *showed up*. The very next day, too. Deryn had been so sure the whole thicker screw thing had been an easy lie to get them out of an awkward situation that he almost knocked a pile of exercise books right off the table when there was a knock and he looked up to see Abel leaning against his doorway.

"Sorry," the man told him, lifting a red toolbox with a faint smile. "Didn't mean to startle you."

"No," Deryn said quickly, pulse still beating madly. "Come in, I..." He stood, glancing around for the desk. No one had been able to make it squeak gratingly all day, but it'd distracted Deryn for another reason instead so he wasn't sure he was really better off than before.

Abel stepped forward and pushed the door shut behind himself for no reason Deryn could see. He headed straight for the desk like he could sense it. Maybe if you were a carpenter, you could. Abel turned to him, smile a little tentative. "I figured you'd be working late again."

Deryn sighed, shrugging and tapped the books on the desk he'd taken over—it helped him stay awake to move around the classroom. "Well, these all need marking."

"What for?" Abel asked companionably as he took out some tools. All manual, Deryn noticed curiously.

"So kids can look at them and see what they did wrong."

That got him a raised eyebrow. "And kids look at them?"

Deryn grimaced. It seemed his unexpected helper wasn't going to pull any punches.

"I try my best," he admitted with a wave of his hand. Marking wasn't so bad, Deryn would take repetitive and pointless over staff meetings any day. At least he could go get a fresh cup of tea or wash his face any time he felt like it.

The carpenter hummed, easily upending the desk to work more comfortably and Deryn dragged his eyes back to the fill-in-the-gaps exercise in front of him. "How long have you been teaching?"

"Two years." He got the green pen and scanned one paragraph, identifying the words the student had filled in from having read them in twenty other books already. He ticked and crossed and gave him the page in their textbook where he could find the verb declensions.

"Right out of uni?" Abel guessed. He was doing something, probably unscrewing, but Deryn wasn't going to look.

University seemed not like another world but another universe, even his initial placement hadn't quite prepared him for the realities of his job. Behaviour was much better back in their small town, at least.

"I have always wanted to teach," he said easily, crossing another sentence in the wrong order. "So I finished my degree and got into the teaching qualification course right away."

"You seem older," Abel told him, absently. It wasn't something people told Deryn often—in fact, he couldn't remember hearing it since he'd been a kid. Abel stopped with the glue in his hands and stole a look, which was when Deryn realised he'd looked up himself. "That's a compliment," he clarified. "Wisdom beyond your years and all that."

Deryn gulped, quickly glancing down. He could feel his face heating up in a manner most decidedly reminiscent of his teenage years. He missed having longer hair to hide behind. "Thank you," he managed.

ABEL

"Must have been nice, knowing what you wanted to do," he said, a little too quickly.

He made sure to keep his eyes fixed on the second screw he was adding directly on the wooden leg to give the table another point of support besides the original joint. It was an old enough piece of furniture to actually be made completely of wood—made to last, but only with appropriate care. And humans had forgotten how to care for things, they'd figured out a way to produce new stuff so cheaply, so they'd just replace whatever broke—never mind that the old stuff just needed a little sanding and paint, or that it'd end up piled up high in a dump site.

The human's heart was still beating a little fast, but he managed to make his voice sound even when he said, "You seem to be doing alright."

"Ah, well, that's now in my old age. I... Well, I didn't handle things so well, back when I was younger." He didn't regret Eve, of course not, but he couldn't forget the pain it'd caused Tristan, the way the notion of staying with the pack and not being able to attend university had seemed to drain him of life. Abel was a simple guy, he could have been happy in his small town with his small job, but Tristan... Tristan had needed something else. Something Abel had always known he couldn't give him.

It wasn't like the attraction had been manufactured by the full moon. At least not for him.

Deryn decided to put him out of his misery, recalling him to the present. "Why did you choose carpentry?"

"Oh, it seemed... I always liked doing things, art was my favourite subject in school, but I liked helping out at home too—fences and all that."

"You guys keep animals?"

The question almost made Abel laugh. Even not counting the wolves themselves, which was debatable, the pack also kept a number of sheep for milk and meat. Once a year, they also purchased a couple of deer, always before spring so as to allow them a plentiful mating season. The years when there were calves were traditionally considered of good fortune by the pack, though now that just meant they got to hunt once more when they were grown. They had to, their ecosystem was not really fit to sustain animals that size after how much land the humans had built on or put to use for harvest.

"Sheep," he said simply. It wasn't that odd in Criccieth, really, but he still felt Deryn's surprise.

"That's very traditional of you," he observed. He was tapping his green pen against his own chin, curious eyes intent on Abel.

"Nothing wrong with tradition," Abel said easily. "You didn't train here, right? Did you go to Cardiff?"

"Manchester," Deryn said. "But I guess I'm pretty traditional, I missed home. Though the city's... Well, it's pretty good if you're a bit odd, I suppose."

"Really?" Abel asked, interested. "I think odd people get on just fine here, we get to pass as eccentric instead of unique or something, but in the end what matters is that people respect you, isn't it? And for that, isn't it better if they know you?"

Deryn gave a small thoughtful nod in response. "Criccieth is not that small, though."

"Nah, but you know your neighbours, don't you?" Abel pointed out. "And you get to sit down with your kid's teacher and talk about your life, do they do that down in Manchester?"

That earned him a laugh, and it turned out those pink lips came with dimples. "Can't say I ever got a parent coming to shout at me for not being enough of a feminist," Deryn conceded. "Maybe they are not as progressive as they make out."

"See? You're better off here." The words that had seemed fine in his head sounded a little too warm when they made it out into the open and Abel gulped and looked back down at the work he'd finished in the space of five minutes. "Well, I'm done with this, so I'm gonna let you work—"

"No," Deryn cut in. "I mean, I said I'd treat you to coffee. I could really use a break. Just need..." He glanced at the pile on his desk. "Ten minutes?"

He sounded so tentative about it that Abel couldn't have said no even if he'd had anything to look forward to but an empty house—it was Eve's day at Tristan's. He'd have been welcomed at their table; Lyall had long ago accepted Abel held no grudge against him for stealing his omega. But they had their own life and they should get to enjoy it without always needing to give him scraps off their table like he was a stray.

He really needed to sort out his social life, learn to be an adult, to reconnect with his friends... Maybe find someone of his own. He glanced around mostly to look away from Deryn. "You mind if I have a look? Maybe there's something else..."

"Of course!" Deryn had a pretty smile, even when he was trying to suppress it. Even if he was only happy that Abel was fixing up his classroom, it was still something to make someone light up like that with just a little manual work.

It suddenly seemed odd to him that his daughter spent so many hours in a room he'd never even examined. There were examples of children's work on the walls and he amused himself by tracking down Eve's without checking the name tags. It'd been a long time since he'd stopped being afraid he'd drop her or traumatize her beyond repair, but he liked to see proof of the person she was out of home—the person she truly was when they weren't there to guide her. From what little French he recalled, he discovered she'd written a paragraph about a celebrity and his boyfriend. Humans had got over the murderous hatred—for the most part—but they were still perfectly content to live in a world where heterosexuality was the only example offered. Was the singer even real?

"Hey," he said before realising he might be interrupting and turning to face the teacher. Deryn was on his feet, jacket halfway down his arms in a way that left his upper arms bulging a little. Abel looked up. "Um, this Adam guy with the boyfriend... Eve was writing about him and I wondered if she made him up."

Deryn snorted, pulling his jacket up his shoulders and shaking his head. "You look way too young to be asking that question."

"Good genes," Abel said simply.

"He is real, though he has been called dreamy," he added and the way his heartbeat skipped said a lot about who might have done the calling.

"Has he?" he teased, taking a step closer. It wasn't like he hadn't felt the pull, but... "By who?"

"Whom," Deryn quipped, mouth pursed and eyes shining. "And fine, me. But you should see him before you judge. He also sings really well."

"So how did he come up in French class?" He followed Deryn towards the door. He'd left his jacket in his car and his car at home since a few miles at a light jog were hardly a stroll for him.

"We try to keep it interesting so we have a few classes on celebrities, there's a lot of material from teen magazines and blogs too, plus if they already know the answers, it's easier for them to figure out what the French means. Those essays are probably the longest they will write all year," he added. "Of course, some of them still don't quite believe we can check for plagiarism so..."

"At least they are reading in French?" Abel offered, holding the door open.

Deryn hesitated, which was another weird human habit—who got into an argument over whose job it was to be polite? "Yeah, the copy and paste sections mostly made sense. Then again, there's also *automatic translation*."

These last words he pronounced like some would a contagious disease that disfigured the sufferer before it killed them slowly, and Abel couldn't contain a laugh. "Hey, it has its place!"

"Like the instructions of how to put together a desk made by modern indentured servants?" Deryn shot back, and reached out and opened the front door for him in turn.

Abel took a step away, purposely widening his eyes. "Wow, get me some coffee before you start the revolution!"

That earned him a sly look. "I thought the revolution was *your* thing."

"I'll share," Abel told him easily. "Once I have caffeine in me."

The café really was close, and it must have been later than he'd thought because it wasn't that busy.

Deryn watched him down a double espresso with wide eyes. "I hope you don't do that in front of your kid," he observed.

"Huh? Why?"

"Role model."

"Are you trying to prove you are more 'woke' than me by hating coffee?" Abel checked, sitting down with a cup of Lady Grey.

"What? No, I just— Sore throat, there's honey in this," Deryn explained, raising his own huge mug of green tea.

Abel had known that, given that he had a nose. "Are you getting sick?" he asked curiously. It wasn't that werewolves never caught anything, but it was rare for a bacteria or virus to get strong enough to overcome their immune system. He wondered if he could catch it from... being close.

Deryn laughed. "Why do you sound like a psychopath when you ask that? I might be getting a bit of a cold, can't afford to get really sick."

"But the school would still pay—"

Deryn waved that away. "Yeah, of course, but they wouldn't do *my job* for me, so when I got back there'd be an insane amount of catching up to do."

"Doesn't sound like you're actually getting to take time off."

"I guess..." He drank, eyelashes fluttering a little in obvious pleasure as he swallowed. "Well, you're a parent, there's no time off for you either, is there?"

"Of course there is! I have my family for that. Right now..." He glanced at the clock. "Eve should be getting homework help from Tristan's boyfriend, who is nineteen, by the way, but a lot better at every subject except maybe art."

Deryn didn't say anything for a long moment, but he forced a smile when Abel offered one of his own. "Um... I guess then I win, being a teacher sucks the most." He sipped, eyes lowered.

It had probably not been the most sensitive thing to say to someone sharing their woes, Abel realised with a wince. "You do enjoy it, though, don't you?"

"Yes," the answer was not long in coming, though for an affirmation it lacked some warmth. "It'll get easier, once I have more resources and I know how to handle things better."

Abel thought that sounded a little vague for a plan. "Was last year worse?"

"Can't compare yet," Deryn objected. "Also, might jinx it if I get overconfident."

For all humans claimed to be enlightened and not to believe in... well, werewolves, for one, it was surprising how often they tried to follow the ancient rules of the universe just in case.

He wondered what Deryn would have thought of him in his fur. He couldn't tell him, of course, and why would he? This was just a friendly chat.

"What about you? How's your job going?"

"Lonely," was the first word to come to mind and out of his mouth. Abel straightened in his seat. "Um, I mean, I love it, the pieces and... just finding a space and changing a whole room with a dinner set or a wooden chest."

"You probably spend most of your day on your own though," Deryn said thoughtfully. He took a long sip of his drink, throat working where he'd removed the yellow scarf that set off his red coat.

Red Riding Hood and the wolf, did the universe have no shame? Abel quickly filled his own mouth with whatever was left in his cup.

Not that Deryn was in any danger, Abel was just looking.

He put down his drink and met Abel's eyes. "You know, sometimes I feel like I do too. I'm surrounded by kids all day and I need some quiet at lunch and... some days I don't talk to an adult at all. Nothing beyond 'good morning' anyway."

But then again, in the story, the one in true danger was the wolf, wasn't he?

Chapter 2

ABEL

"...B ut Mr Deryn says it's fine."

Top Gun was on, which was normally just background noise, but he must have been paying more attention than he thought to the car babble because the name brought him up short. He probably shouldn't have muted the telly and made it obvious he hadn't been listening, though.

Eve gave him a suspicious look. "What?"

"Mr Deryn..." Abel repeated. "He's a good teacher, isn't he?"

"Oh my god, how do you know him?" she asked at once, eyes widening and heart picking up. "Did you *complain*? About that stupid St Valentine's thing?" She was already on her feet, dropping her open exercise book on the coffee table between the telly and the sofa. "He's *the best* teacher and now he'll think I— You said you wouldn't!" she accused, voice growing a little shrill.

Abel stared at her, too stunned by the strength of her reaction to come up with a response.

Tristan would have cut her off and reminded her to mind her tone—maybe his ex wasn't a fan of the hierarchy of alphas and omegas but he definitely expected their daughter to respect her elders. But Abel just watched her, concentrating on calming himself down as she worked herself up over his imagined misdeeds.

Eve was dramatic, but she wasn't oblivious so it wasn't long before she demanded, "Why aren't you saying anything?"

"Will you listen?" Abel asked her.

She huffed and crossed her arms, pressing her lips together.

He thought about making her say it, but then decided it didn't matter. "You're overreacting. I did go to speak to him because you had chess last Wednesday when I went to pick you up, but all that happened was that we had a chat and I fixed one of the desks in his classroom." He hesitated, because that wasn't all of it, of course, he'd gone back the next day and they'd spent at least an hour chatting over coffee, but... Well, Eve was hardly in the mood to be reasonable, he could tell her about it later.

"A chat?"

He gave her a wide-eyed look of confusion. "A conversation?" he told her. "An exchange of ideas? Natter? Chinwag?"

Her lips were parted and when she finally spoke again, she sounded dubious but not confrontational. "You're making those up."

"Nope," Abel said with relish, waiting a moment so she'd hear his steady heartbeat.

She huffed, rolling her eyes. "Whatever."

Abel managed to hold back a laugh until she was out of the room.

DERYN

The new boyfriend actually explained a lot about Abel. It could still be an open relationship situation, but the way Abel had spoken of this young man and called him better had been painful to hear. Considering Eve was thirteen, Tristan had to be close to Abel's age, what was he doing dating a kid barely out of school?

Deryn still regretted not telling Abel being good in school didn't make this new guy better than him. But to be fair he'd been repressing most of the positive things he wanted to tell Abel since they'd met. It'd seemed too much like flirting, if his rather uncouth attempts could be called that, and he'd thought...

That Abel was taken.

Not that it changed anything if he wasn't, obviously. He was still gorgeous and older and probably nursing a broken heart after his husband had left him for a younger man.

Maybe he could say something later, or just ask about it to show he was listening. When his friends had been around, he'd always been a good friend. Back when dating had seemed completely impossible, it'd been something he'd told himself, that he loved others and was loved in return.

Deryn had no idea what he was doing, but Abel showed up again the next week on Wednesday (chess club) and Thursday (Tristan's day with Eve). He brought along his computer to work on his expenses and they sat in the chilly room—Abel still wasn't wearing a jacket—in companionable silence as they got their work done.

"Aren't you cold?" Deryn asked when he was done with his marking. It only occurred to him a moment too late that he might be interrupting, but the other man looked up like he'd been expecting a question.

"No, I run warm."

Deryn sensibly didn't attempt to confirm that statement by placing his hand either on Abel's stubbled cheek—some days were better than others, but he'd never seen him without some facial hair—or on the line of his neck his shirt collar left exposed.

Damn, he needed to get laid. Even if it left him feeling slightly queasy, it'd still be better than the way his eyes kept wandering. He closed his books. "I'm done. Coffee?"

"I'm paying," Abel warned him on the way over.

Deryn rolled his eyes at him, he'd figured he'd left chivalry behind at least, but of course modernity had made everything more complicated. "Weren't you just looking at your expenses? Didn't that inspire you to save?"

The older man snorted. "Coffee is not an expense, otherwise I'd be running in the red. And I don't mind paying for good materials sourced from certified providers."

He held the door open and Abel went through without a comment. That was something, he thought with a smile. "Can you really trust those certificates though? I mean, I just look at them for food and I always wonder..."

"If they aren't selling you a clear conscience?" Abel finished.

"Well, yeah."

Abel was frowning a little, but he didn't seem annoyed, which was the reaction Deryn normally got when he questioned whether someone paying twice the going price for vegetables actually knew if they had really been cultivated responsibly both socially and ecologically.

"What do you want to drink?" Abel checked, tilting his head towards the till, reminding Deryn there was a goal besides finding a reason to talk a little longer.

"Latte, please."

"I can feel it in the wood," Abel said, setting the tray on the table.

Deryn blinked at him, at a loss. "What?"

"The wood," Abel repeated, and Deryn finally caught on. "It feels different when it comes from somewhere where they treated it well. You know that experiment they did? With the two plants that got insulted or praised for a year?"

Deryn shook his head, reaching for a packet of sugar but just fiddling with it. Abel's eyes were a little far away, blue like a summer afternoon sky—half the colour from the sea—and then he shrugged and met Deryn's eyes again and Deryn almost choked on air.

"It's not super scientific, I guess, but they put two identical plants in a hall with a sign that said either 'praise me' or 'insult me' and after, like, six months, the 'bad' plant had withered while the other flourished."

"Seriously?" He knew he was frowning a little incredulously, it was just that he wasn't given to... well, believe in magic or whatever the new age equivalent was.

"Yeah, and it makes sense." Abel was nodding, quietly sharing his thoughts, obviously unconcerned if it made him look strange. "Nothing exists in a void, so I figure... the trees that are surrounded by people who care, who know maybe that their progeny will live on and their land will prosper..." He paused, seeking Deryn's eyes again.

Deryn yanked his eyes away from the openness on his face almost as fast as he yanked his phone out of his pocket. "I need to see this," he explained. The connection was a little slow, but he didn't look up as it loaded. He really hoped he wasn't blushing.

He wasn't completely sure if the video evidence was strict enough for a science experiment, but it made sense to him. And it got more interesting still when it turned out a school teacher had taken their students to see the plants and record messages for them. "Oh, bullying, this is... I have to use this class..." he said, fingers twitching for a pen. He settled for emailing himself the link.

And then Abel laughed, his joy making Deryn's breath hitch. "Bit of a workaholic, are you?" he asked, and Deryn felt his weight against the table between them, almost enough to make him peek if he hadn't been ready to resist.

He had no idea why it was so hard. They hardly knew each other, didn't they? And Abel was handsome, sure, but it wasn't like Deryn had grown up in a convent or something...

He shrugged, clicking on another link and hoping he wasn't being completely obvious.

The final result was indeed a wilted fern who'd been battered with negativity and a flourishing one that had been praised lovingly. His aunt had always talked to her plants, he remembered suddenly, she'd insisted it did them good.

There were more videos—an infinity of them most likely—but Deryn made himself put the phone down and look up at his... friend? He could use the word, he supposed. "This is fantastic," he told him, and reached for his coffee at last. It'd keep his mouth full for a minute.

He completely forgot he'd never added sugar and he swallowed his mouthful with a grimace that made his companion laugh again.

"You really get lost in it, don't you?"

"You're the one who told me about it, Mr Indifferent," Deryn reminded him, opening three packets at once and pouring them into his cup—Abel had got him the large one for some reason—he'd need to pee twice before he could finish it. "I'm just thinking of making my lessons more engaging."

"No, I— It's nice to see you love what you do. It looks like a lot of work, lots of paper cuts," he added with a lighter lilt. "But I would have loved to learn about this stuff in school."

"Back in the Middle Ages?" Deryn asked, which was probably a bit rude except of course Abel looked like a bloody model and definitely not old enough to have a teenage kid.

"Subtle, kid," Abel told him, mouth quirking into a half smile. "I'm thirty-three."

Nine years older than Deryn himself. Not that it mattered, of course.

ABEL

Deryn had had a pile of books on his table when he'd arrived.

It was Wednesday again, but he wasn't picking up Eve. She was going to the city centre with friends after chess club.

Not that he needed to mention that to Deryn, or maybe he could, once it got late enough to be relevant. He was almost sure Deryn wouldn't ask if Abel was there just to spend time with him.

If Deryn hadn't been human, Abel would have thought he'd given himself away.

Of course, Tristan wasn't human and while he was normally distracted with his work, he had noticed Abel had declined three dinner invitations in a row.

"Is it... I mean, you and Lyall are fine, aren't you?"

He'd sounded so genuinely worried that Abel hadn't had the heart to do anything but tell the truth. "I'm not avoiding you guys, I... I'm meeting someone tomorrow, so I have to finish a piece now or I'll fall behind." In the last few weeks, he'd actually caught up with all his paperwork so overall, working with Deryn helped—even if he got a little distracted sometimes.

"Oh." Tristan nodded, looking pensive. Of course, he wouldn't want to pry, it didn't matter that Abel and he knew each other better than anyone else in the world—and Tristan's new boyfriend didn't change thirty years of friendship. "Good," he said, nodding more decisively than the word justified. "You should have fun."

Maybe Tristan thought he had a date, so what? A meeting with a friend wasn't that far off. Deryn was beautiful and he knew Abel liked men, and he was choosing to spend hours with him. And it could have been a sign of something... different. But Deryn was just nice, nothing more, and he was human, of course, which was why even contemplating anything but nice afternoons sharing coffee and trivia was absurd.

Maybe the world was obsessed with romance, but Abel was smart enough to know he'd found something precious. Small, but necessary, the kind of thing that made days better and lightened your load.

It wasn't settling to take what was on offer, it was just common sense.

Abel was happy to.

"You never showed me those pictures," he reminded Deryn as he set up his sketchpad. He hadn't had the time to create sketches for his catalogue in ages, probably because any time he'd wanted to, he'd felt like he'd needed to file his expenses properly and ended up doing neither.

The kind of wildly intricate work he loved best was not really fit for anyone that wasn't an aristocrat or a tech billionaire, both of which were scarce in Criccieth. But hey, a guy needed a hobby, even if that hobby was also kind of his job.

"Oh, yeah, lemme..." Deryn grabbed for his phone and started scrolling. He had small, dexterous hands. Well-suited to working with something as small as tweezers, really. But as he watched, Deryn made an unhappy sound, then exhaled slowly. "I can't..."

"Can't find them? Don't—"

"No," Deryn cut in, voice going a little rough. "I *always* take pictures, sometimes even in the middle of it just so... But there's nothing, I haven't done anything in at least two months..." He glanced up, heart beating too fast, eyes crinkled with what seemed real worry.

"You don't have to," Abel gently pointed out.

"But I *want* to," Deryn replied, low and tired. He looked both older and younger with his suddenly open expression and Abel couldn't help himself, he reached for his hand.

His pulse skipped at that, right next to Abel's index finger, and Abel had to bite his tongue not to make a noise. But Deryn didn't pull back and Abel didn't let go. He gulped and forced himself to focus. He wasn't going to fall down on the job as a friend just because he maybe had a little crush.

"Time is love," Abel said simply. "And you love your job, don't you?"

"I'd like to love something else besides my job," Deryn shot back, tense and unhappy. For a moment, it seemed impossible to look away, but then Deryn relaxed with a sigh. "I'm sorry. I just really wanted to show you."

It seemed safe to let go, and yet... He did it, but he had to take up his cup so he wouldn't try to take it back. "Have you sold them?"

"What?" He thought Deryn's eyes were following his hand as it retreated, but that could have been anything, really. A reflex, or...

"The sculptures," Abel clarified. "Did you give them to someone?"

Deryn shook his head, a wild curl bouncing as he did. "No, they're at home."

For a moment, he couldn't speak because all he wanted was to ask. Can I come with you and see them? And he wasn't fooling himself, much less...

"There you go," he managed at last, "Easy enough fix then."

Deryn's eyes flickered up to him, and his pulse got a little wild again. But he just nodded. "I'll bring them over next time," he promised.

DERYN

He was just seeing what he wanted to be true. Letting his little crush get out of hand because Abel had held his hand for a minute to comfort him when he'd been upset like... Like he was desperately lonely, which he was.

Abel was lonely too, and brave enough to say it, even, and Deryn was happy to help alleviate that a little. He just needed to make sure he didn't let the multicoloured heart-shaped decorations get to him.

It was for the best, of course, how would that even work? Maybe Abel wasn't married anymore, but he had been, and Deryn... Deryn had barely managed to keep his last boyfriend from breaking up with him in the middle of exam season at uni.

Nine years wasn't that much in the grand scheme of things, maybe, but Deryn's inexperience was.

Even knowing that, he was still nervous about Abel seeing the sculptures. They'd taken him so long and if he just said something polite to be nice... Well, it'd make sense, Abel did carvings on wood so beautiful people were willing to wait months and pay a small fortune to get them, what was a hummingbird compared to that?

And it'd been so long since someone *had* been nice, and interested, taken the time to talk to him... Maybe it wouldn't be so bad if that's all he got.

He opened the box and set the lid aside, not looking up as he took out the first of the sculptures, encased in a simple wooden frame. Not until Abel let out a little sigh.

"Oh." Abel's eyes were stuck to the object he held and his big hand was stretched towards the frame, suspended in mid-air as he watched. "This is *paper*?" he demanded in a whisper.

Deryn had to swallow. He put the sculpture down on the table between them, as if Abel's attention would transfer to it and away from him. "Well, there's some blue tack and glue in there too, but mostly paper."

Abel glanced up, eyes glinting, and asked, "May I?"

The formality made something in Deryn's chest tighten. It was crazy to react like that to a little show of respect, but Abel's whole demeanour seemed to have shifted. It was too much for... But he wouldn't go to all this trouble of pretending, would he? Deryn tried to remember if he'd ever made any type of effort to be conciliatory that hadn't been clearly and transparently just that.

He couldn't; Abel didn't do subtlety, which was how Deryn knew the soft looks and the continued visits didn't mean what he wanted them to. No, not wanted, just... Anyway, Abel was just kind and a little lonely; his kid was growing up, his partner had left him, and he'd never mentioned any friends.

When offered it, Abel took the frame like it was made of the most fragile of porcelains, movements slow and measured. The hummingbird wasn't white like the instructions had suggested—Deryn simply hadn't been able to resist adding a little colour, just some orange on the tail and the head, but it still wasn't quite...

"The colour really adds depth," Abel offered. "Man, how long did this take you?"

"Um, well, it's not... you get the hang of it so a couple hours, maybe."

Abel shook his head, not looking away from the tiny paper bird and even though he wasn't looking at Deryn, maybe precisely *because* he wasn't looking at Deryn, not at his face at least, but at something deeper, something he'd *chosen*... He found he couldn't speak.

He took the next one out of the box instead. Another bird, an eagle, not delicate like the hummingbird but almost violent and that had been what had worried Deryn the most as he'd put it together, that he'd somehow lose that quality of wildness to it. It wasn't quite like the original, but he could see that edge in it, and he was proud of the speck of gold—half a grain of rice painted with marker—he'd used for the eye.

"The paper wouldn't go your way in that corner," Abel observed, nothing judgemental about it, just a fact. Like he really imagined the paper to have a mind of its own.

Not that Deryn hadn't cursed his materials before.

Maybe there was some... spirit in it still, like the fern trees, even after they were dead and processed into pulp and put together again.

"I think maybe I didn't mark the fold well enough," he admitted.

"Mmm... could be. It's still beautiful, in a way it kinda makes sense, an eagle wouldn't just let you move it around, would it?" He looked up with a smile too full of mischief for a grown man.

Deryn stared at him, fascinated and overwhelmed and touched all at once.

He took out another piece, even though it was absurd to imagine baring himself further could in any way help him feel *less* overwhelmed.

Abel was complimentary, taking his time with each, sometimes reaching for another frame to compare the texture or the tridimensionality.

Deryn let him, he didn't know what else to do. None of the people he'd slept with had ever touched *him* with this much care. And it was crazy, of course, he wasn't made of glass and paper, held in place by a little glue and his own inherent lightness...

But he wanted it.

As unwisely and hopelessly as he wanted Abel.

"This one is lovely," his friend said, not bothering to disguise the pleasure in his voice. Why should he? Any artist would want their work complimented, even if most of that work had been copied off others and wasn't really...

"I take it you like wolves?" Abel's eyes shone enough to make Deryn realise the sun had gone down and he hadn't done any marking since his guest had arrived.

Deryn nodded, shrugging a little. "Who doesn't? They are beautiful and I love the idea of packs, strength in numbers... Dunno," he added. "Guess it's a bit romantic of me."

"Nah," Abel said. "Humans could learn some lessons from pack animals," he suggested with a smile that Deryn didn't understand but could not look away from.

"Yeah," he conceded. "It'd be nice if people stayed in one place, for one thing. Like, all my friends from school have left town."

Abel's expression softened. "Do they come visit?"

"Well, yeah, their parents are here, but it's not the same. I— It wasn't what I imagined when I decided to apply for a job here."

Abel's lips parted, tongue briefly peeking out, but then he glanced back at the wolf. "Never go back to a place where you have been happy, right?"

"I guess I should have listened to the advice of more bookshop mugs," Deryn told him sardonically.

It came out a little sharp, but Abel just snorted. "You cannot deny the wisdom of porcelain," he declared.

When he excused himself to go to the loo, Deryn was grateful for the reprieve.

He started packing but then, when it was the wolf's turn, he set it aside instead. Maybe Abel would want to keep it, and that would certainly make more sense than hanging it around his small flat, which was already getting crowded with his other projects.

ABEL

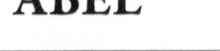

He'd been looking forward to having another look at the sculptures, but he wasn't surprised that Deryn had packed them away. He was used to selling his own art and sometimes it was still a little uncomfortable to have another person look at it. By now he was pretty sure Deryn hadn't shown his work to anyone outside the internet, if that.

Of course, it could be that it was almost six and Abel had kept him from catching up with marking while he browsed. If he kept it up, they'd have to miss their coffee.

And then he took a step closer and something that wasn't Deryn caught his attention. He turned his head. The wolf sculpture was sitting on the edge of the desk, carefully casual next to the embroidered box Deryn had brought it along in. But the only one still out.

"What's up with this little guy?" he asked, sitting back down on the chair on the other side of the desk from Deryn. The desk was quite small and their knees had brushed together a couple of times. And there was no reason for Abel to care since he didn't live in a Victorian novel.

"Oh, nothing," Deryn said at once. Abel didn't think he'd been really checking the book open in front of him. "It's... I thought maybe..." His golden eyes flickered up and he shrugged, dark eyelashes brushing winter pale skin. "You could take it, if you want."

"Seriously?" Abel asked and it must have sounded wrong because Deryn stiffened, heart jumping. "I would love that!" he added perhaps a little too effusively, but he couldn't let him imagine... He wanted to touch him again, but that wouldn't be... He reached for the gift he had been offered instead. "I can't believe you'd part with this. You could sell them, you know?"

Deryn's eyes returned to his face, still cautious but beginning to smile. "A good side hustle to save for pension?"

Abel laughed, too loud and too long but he couldn't stop. His thumbs were fascinated by the texture of the untreated wood under his fingertips and his eyes were feasting on the glow of Deryn's happiness. "Can't ever be too prudent!" he declared in his best impression of his grandfather, who was pushing on a hundred and fifty and still wouldn't quite shut up in pack meetings about the dangers of humans.

Deryn joined him, chuckling.

"You haven't said thank you," he pointed out when he'd calmed down, one eyebrow up to make it clear it wasn't a real reprimand.

"My mum would be so disappointed," Abel dramatized, then let his smile go and reached out for Deryn's arm, covered in cotton and wool but still warm with life under his fingers. He squeezed, just once, but he let his fingers rest there as he said, "Thank you, Deryn, I love my Valentine's present."

The other man's eyes widened and his heart jumped. He was flushing too, painfully obvious over his pale cheeks, like a painting in pastels of a young child, red lipped and dark haired, eye bright with mirth.

Except of course there was nothing innocent or childish about the way Deryn was watching him now, was there?

Abel would have leaned in right then and there.

And then Deryn pulled his arm away, standing. "You're welcome," he said a little tightly. Bewilderingly. He'd been so happy a moment ago, so...

But Abel couldn't ask, could he? One didn't ask why when the answer was no.

"I'll check the cupboard," he announced as Deryn retreated behind the big desk at the back of the room, actually designed for an adult, big enough their knees would have never brushed under it. "Been meaning to."

Deryn had never sat at it in his presence before.

Deryn didn't object and once he'd turned away, Abel allowed his eyes to close and his feelings to come onto his face for a moment. Once he did this last bit of work, maybe he could skip his next visit, give himself a bit of a break, or...

Or he could ask. Actually asking couldn't be too much, could it? Just the once, just so he could make sense of the looks and the warmth and this sudden retreat.

Or not, just so he would *know*.

He could deal with rejection; he'd learned that early on.

He must have been really lost in thought because Deryn's voice behind him startled him enough he jumped, elbow going straight into the shelf behind him and sending its contents raining down on him. He gritted his teeth against the flash of pain. And then he was being yanked forward and away from the deluge of pens and glue sticks.

When he blinked next, Deryn's hands were around his wrists and the younger man was looking up at him, no barriers between them. "You okay?" Up close, his eyelashes were thick and soft looking. His heart was beating wildly.

As was Abel's.

The hands around his wrists were warm and too small to reach all the way around, but that hadn't mattered to Deryn—he hadn't hesitated to pull him to safety.

Abel didn't hesitate either, not a single thought required as he leaned down and pressed his mouth to Deryn's cheek, close enough to his mouth so as to almost not matter. It was soft and warm under his lips, only a hint of stubble, Deryn's breath hitching, his fingers tightening their hold.

His mouth parted under Abel's, a chain reaction that couldn't be stopped, his tongue coming out, his hands climbing to tug his shoulders down, Abel's arms finding their way around him and bringing him closer, both of them stumbling a little but not falling—too close together to fall.

Deryn was light, easy to move when Abel stepped forward and pressed him against the door, a move so fluid it could have almost been choreographed. The next step brought Deryn's hips up, arching into him, welcoming and eager so that Abel couldn't have said for certain if he'd pressed his knee forward or Deryn had pulled it there. The tender breathless whimper that got him made that immaterial.

Abel pushed again, sucking on Deryn's earlobe as he exposed his throat in a way that made his wolf howl inside him. It wasn't the same, it didn't mean... but it didn't seem to matter when Deryn shuddered hard enough Abel's fingers instinctively dug into his hips to keep him in place.

With the door at his back and Abel plastered to his front, there was nowhere for him to go, and he gave no sign of wanting to get away, hips shoving forward in tight little circles, crotch hot and... God, *his scent—salty and spicy and so...* Abel groaned, trembling in his arms as Deryn rubbed himself against his thigh, burning despite the layers of clothing and hard too. And Abel had to *feel* that wetness, the heat of him...

And then, like a shock to the system, a door closed too loudly in the corridor and he jerked back, almost falling in his haste to get away. *What the hell...?*

Deryn's eyes, the gold eclipsed by his arousal, met his, dazed and beautiful, too much emotion to determine what he was feeling. His lips were redder than usual, a mark Abel hadn't intended to leave and could almost not resist. "Sorry," he said, even as he dug his nails into his own hands to keep himself still.

The word was like a spell. "Oh, I—" Deryn glanced around, standing straight and stepping away from the door. "That was..." He shook his head, glancing around as if his composure had simply been misplaced. "Inappropriate," he settled on.

"Yes!" Abel quickly agreed. "I... I'm sorry," he repeated, and tried to prove it by taking a further step away from Deryn. He almost fell when he ran into a desk because he wasn't quite able to look away.

Deryn's laughter shocked him a little. "Are you trying to make me catch you again?"

Abel glanced up, smile already blooming. "Nah, wouldn't use the same trick twice."

Deryn's smile wobbled and he swallowed audibly, for Abel at least. He was worried, and he still met Abel's eyes head on. "You really...?"

He didn't specify, but Abel was beginning to think it didn't matter.

"I really," Abel told him simply.

"Mr Deryn?" Someone called out from the corridor and Abel instinctively took another step back to let him pass despite the two meters already between them. Deryn returned the greeting a little too cheerfully.

It was one of the cleaners. They hadn't even knocked, but why would they? Deryn was supposed to be marking student books. Because this was a *school*. Abel stoically kept back another apology.

"I am done with this," he said instead, covering up. "Should we catch up later about the desk?"

For a moment, Deryn didn't reply, but when Abel braved another look, he realised it was because he was pressing his lips together, eyes bright with repressed laughter. "Sure," he managed.

Abel nodded and turned towards the door, feeling a little bit like he was floating.

He was on cloud nine for exactly fifteen minutes, then, in his car on the way to pick up some groceries, he remembered a little fact: Deryn was human. He'd hooked up with humans before, and no one even cared much unless someone got pregnant, but a relationship... A relationship meant telling the truth.

The truth his whole species had closely guarded for centuries to protect themselves from human fear and as of late, their obsession with cutting up anything that interested them to see how it ticked.

Deryn would never... But he didn't think even an Alpha as permissive as Mary would let him risk it.

It probably said something about Abel that the only person he could imagine himself talking to about this was his ex. Or maybe it said something about Tristan.

Sex and relationship therapy was pretty much Tristan's job, after all, even if he mostly lectured instead of talking to people one on one. He was also the one person in his pack Abel knew for certain wouldn't judge him for feeling the way he did.

The groceries would have to wait. One of the perks of having a teenager at home was that she would certainly not complain about having frozen pizza for the third time that week.

Tristan was understandably surprised to see him on the one day when he *wasn't* supposed to be around, but it turned out Eve and Lyall had started watching a TV show about graphic design together.

"I'm happy to get out of it," Tristan admitted in a whisper, taking hold of his arm and dragging him inside.

On the way to Tristan's studio, Abel caught the sounds of rapid conversation—Eve's voice standing out to him despite all the background noise. He wondered if Deryn and Eve would...

The studio was also the spare bedroom where Abel had slept when he'd stayed over—neither of them were sure if Eve had known they'd sometimes had sex, but they had wanted to make it clear there were absolutely no chances of them ever getting together.

"Abel, what's going on?" his friend asked, and a cup of tea seemed to materialize in front of him.

Abel inhaled deeply. "You know I said I have been... seeing someone?"

Tristan made an affirmative sound.

Abel exhaled. "I met Eve's teacher. Um, French and Spanish teacher," he clarified as if that was relevant. Tristan nodded but let the silence stand. "He was organizing this St Valentine's week thing and it seemed so silly to waste so much time cutting paper hearts and all that..." He trailed off.

"But you like him?" his old friend guessed.

It wasn't much, but it helped to be able to nod. "He's... he's passionate about teaching, and creative, does these incredible sculptures." His fingers twitched and he almost wanted to run to his car and get the wolf. He made himself stay in his seat and meet Tristan's calm gaze. "And he liked that experiment with the plants at Ikea, so he used it for a lesson. And, I mean, we only had coffee a few times, but..." He pressed his fingers to his eyelids, hiding his burning face as much as he could. "I kissed him. Proper made out in his *classroom*."

"Abel," Tristan chided. "Just... you stopped, right? Because Eve—"

"Oh, god, don't!" he begged.

Tristan took pity on him. "Okay, so you stopped," he decided.

Abel nodded, but didn't look at him.

"But he doesn't know."

Despite how obvious they were, the words seemed to cut through him, sharp and unbearable. He shook his head, teeth gritted, heart clenching.

Tristan's hand landed on his shoulder, squeezing gently. "Hey, don't panic."

"But I can't—" Abel started to say, terror suddenly rising in his throat, and he didn't know why because of course he couldn't tell a human what he was. What *they* were, it went specifically against the laws that protected the packs.

Maybe there weren't werewolf hunters any longer, but now there were scientists who would happily disappear them into an underground lab to figure out what made them live longer and age slower. And if it'd just been his life, he could have—

"Shhh," Tristan instructed, as uncaring of his omega orientation as always. He cupped Abel's cheek and forced his chin up. "There's always a way."

Abel frowned. "Tristan, what way? It's forbidden, how—"

"Abe," Tristan's fingers tightened, his voice growing deeper. "I've never—" He glanced down. "I know you think I don't pay attention, but in the last few weeks you've been... happy, I guess. You're always smiling. Well, when you're here," he gently chided, tugging at a stray lock of Abel's hair with the glee of a guy who knew his own was too short to be at risk. "But now I get where you went. I actually think I haven't seen you this happy in years, not since..."

"Not since we were kids?" Abel offered, meeting his eyes head on. "You can talk about it; you know I've been over it for ages."

"But there's never been anyone else?" Tristan checked.

"You're pretty hard to replace," Abel told him with a sad smile. He hadn't been trying particularly hard, either. It had never seemed possible to manufacture what had fallen in his lap by accident when Tristan had decided he liked Abel enough to sit next to him in the history lessons that were the first schooling young wolves received.

And even after it'd been over, after he'd understood that for Tristan it had never been as intense as for him, *Abel* had still known what it was like, to hold someone you loved close and push them over the edge.

He'd made do, but he'd never seriously imagined he could find it again.

And how could he really know he had? He'd only known Deryn for a few weeks, after all.

"Do you trust him?" Tristan asked.

"Yes," the answer was past his lips before the question had stopped echoing in the air. He frowned. "I mean, he's... he wouldn't... He really wants to help people. He keeps trying to think of ways to make things easier, more interesting. He would never do anything that could hurt us."

"Then you should tell him."

"Just because I want to, it doesn't mean—"

"Eve," his ex told him simply.

"What?"

"Eve is underage, if she gives herself away and we need to reveal the truth to her teacher to keep him from reporting her, that would be in the pack's best interests. It's been done," he assured Abel when he didn't immediately agree.

"You want me to use Eve to...?"

"Use her?" Tristan repeated, exasperated. "I want you to *ask* her. She can say no, but I don't see why she would. I want to protect her, but shouldn't she know we trust her to help us too when we need her? That's what pack means."

Abel opened his mouth, but he closed it again before he asked Tristan if he was absolutely certain there would be no risk for her.

He was sure Tristan wouldn't slap him, but that didn't mean Abel shouldn't make an effort not to deserve it.

DERYN

Deryn stared at him, dressed up to the nines and standing in his classroom—door closed but still so far from where Deryn sat at one of the student's desks. It was Friday, and despite the kiss they'd shared, Deryn had somehow convinced himself he'd have to wait a week for more.

He couldn't stop his eyes from tracing the lines of the suit. If it was meant to distract him, it was working.

"I don't have your number," Abel explained with a grimace.

Deryn stood up. "Oh, I—"

Abel didn't let him finish. "First, I know I fucked up."

Deryn tensed, but when he opened his mouth, Abel raised a hand to ask for silence.

"I should have never kissed you here." He shook his head. "I'm really embarrassed, and I realise it could have got you fired, or..."

He trailed off, and Deryn suddenly remembered *he* had been worried about this himself. But he'd forgotten, because he'd been thinking about Abel, about the kiss.

It was either romantic or pathetic.

"I kissed you back," he pointed out because he wasn't going to take the out. He was an adult and he could handle his own fuckups.

"Yeah." Abel glanced up, eyes searching his face for an answer Deryn didn't have. "That's why—Well, I was hoping we could do this properly. Dinner or—"

"Yes!" he cut in because if he had to wait one second longer, he was going to burst.

But of course they were *still* in his workplace and he could only stare as Abel's eyes widened.

"Is that why...?" he asked, gesturing at Abel's clothes when he managed to get enough saliva in his dry mouth to speak.

Abel looked down at himself like he'd forgotten he was wearing clothes at all, let alone a suit that looked expensive. "Um, well, yes," he admitted, and damn, Deryn could have sworn he was blushing a little. His long blond hair was a lot neater than usual, too, he noticed.

"Okay," he said again, needlessly, but there weren't many words one could say while grinning like a lunatic.

"Only..." Abel shifted in place, clearly uncomfortable. Deryn didn't think it was the suit. "Would you come home with me?"

Deryn's heart jumped and other parts of him were not unaffected, he was suddenly grateful there was furniture between them. "Um, what?"

"I know, it's— Not to—" Abel cut himself off, glancing around nervously like he expected to get busted. "I have to show you something, before you say yes."

"I said yes already," Deryn reminded him.

But Abel's expression was almost pained. "That's why, you need to know."

It was only then that it crossed Deryn's mind that *he* had something to tell Abel too. He'd been so busy convincing himself the other man was out of his league that he'd forgotten the very real reason a lot of men didn't...

"Okay," he told Abel almost before he could think it through. It was the least he could do, having been on the other side of this conversation before.

ABEL

Deryn had agreed to come with him, and the fact that he'd taken his own car was in no way a bad sign. In fact, if he reacted badly, Abel *wanted* him to be able to get away. The idea of frightening someone he cared for was nauseating, and he'd have done anything to ensure it ended as quickly as humanly possible.

Humanly. Would Deryn still think of him as human when he knew?

If his van had been a bike, Abel would have dropped it on the driveway, uncaring of the likelihood of snow in February. As it was, he stopped in front of his own driveway and got out, exhaling in relief when he spotted Deryn's blue Seat Ibiza right behind him. There was just enough room to fit the smaller car next to his own, for which Abel had to thank his hindbrain and Deryn's skills.

Deryn peeked out and glanced up at the house, heart picking up. The house was right on the edge of pack territory since Abel mostly worked for humans. For a pack house, it was not even that old, and Abel had been glad to buy it from one of his own great grand aunts when she'd wanted to go stay with her brother closer to the forest.

"Wow," Deryn said into the wind. "That's... You live alone?" he checked.

"No, but Eve is at Tristan's," Abel explained.

Deryn jumped. "Oh, of course, sorry, I—" He gestured at the building. "This is... impressive."

His awe made Abel smile. "Come on in." He was still nervous, but it did cross his mind to joke that Deryn would be even more impressed with his *other* assets.

He made tea, because he was British and it was cold and in any case, it seemed a lot less likely someone could freak out while sipping a soothing herbal mix of green tea and fennel—which maybe Abel was a bit creepy for buying after Deryn had ordered it twice in a row during their coffee dates. He was pretty sure he was allowed to call them that now.

Deryn seemed fascinated with his kitchen, which wasn't something Abel could precisely object to considering he'd made every single piece of furniture in it, but it wasn't the time. "Listen, I— I have to tell you something. A secret," he added.

That got him the other man's attention. "Okay, I won't tell." His pulse was a little fast, but steady.

Abel could have asked for more, for him to swear, tried to explain how dangerous a secret it was... But trust wasn't an equation.

He swallowed and opened up, "I'm a werewolf."

Deryn's face froze on the sympathetic expression for a moment, then he frowned. "Is this— Are you... trying to make this cute or something?"

Abel shook his head. "No, I'm serious. I can show you."

"Sh—Show me?" He snorted, but instead of getting up and getting the hell out, he took a long drink from his cup, perhaps an instinct more ingrained than anything the Moon had bestowed upon Abel's people. "Okay, you know what? Go ahead and show me."

Abel stood, a little torn, not because... Well, not because he minded Deryn seeing him in fur, unless *Deryn* turned out to mind.

He licked his lips, glancing down. Why the fuck had he worn his only suit? "I have to undress," he explained.

That made Deryn burst out laughing, porcelain clicking against the plate in a way his great grand aunt would have probably have had a fit about.

Abel could see his point, though, under the circumstances.

"Sure," Deryn managed, gulping hard and rubbing at his eyes like he was actually wiping away tears. "Not like..." He bit his lip and gestured up and down Abel's body. "Not like I mind."

There were two ways to go about this—fast or slow. Abel removed his suit jacket with care, but it was impossible to miss the way Deryn had gone still and attentive, his pulse picking up, his scent intensifying.

Fast it was.

He ignored Deryn's little gasp as he sped up past what a human could have managed, focusing on his task wholeheartedly.

When he glanced up, as bare as he could physically get, Deryn had a hand over his own eyes. He was also breathing a little too fast for someone sitting, and his scent had gone... *Dangerous*, that was the word because right now, Abel couldn't take what was being offered, not under false pretences.

He considered asking him to watch, but he wasn't sure *he* could take it.

When he called, the wolf came forth at once, joyful and excited. It'd wanted to smell Deryn properly for ages and once the fur had fully grown—fast enough it was probably imperceptible for a human, even one who was actually watching—Abel found himself confidently stepping forward and nuzzling at Deryn's knee.

Deryn startled, almost falling off his chair. His eyes were wide as plates and his heart was like cymbals to Abel's wolf hearing. "Oh, fuck."

Abel rubbed his cheek against Deryn's thigh in what he hoped was a comforting move. His scent was strongest there.

"Abel?" Deryn's voice was only a thread, but Abel looked up at once. "If this is a prank, I gotta say..." There were tears in his eyes and Abel couldn't hold back a whimper, to see his mate like that, to... He yanked back, not moving but curling forward as the change rippled through him once more. It ached a little, like an overused muscle, and he was left panting at Deryn's feet.

"Fucking hell," Deryn whispered, like all one needed to do to get him swearing like a sailor was take him out of his classroom (and introduce him to the existence of supernatural creatures, but whatever). Abel was about to speak, to apologize again maybe, when he felt Deryn's deft fingers on his head, untangling his hair, petting softly. "Are you okay? Does that hurt?"

Abel lifted his head, slowly enough Deryn wouldn't let go. "Not..." He coughed a little, swallowing hard, somehow he'd got hair in his mouth, of course. "Not normally, did it too fast."

Deryn was watching him like he'd never seen him before, which wasn't what Abel wanted from him. But at least he was still here, wasn't he? His thumb felt like a brand on Abel's scalp and it was hard not to push back and beg for more.

"You're a werewolf," Deryn told him, almost evenly.

"Yeah," Abel agreed, swallowing. He was starting to feel quite naked and his kitchen tile wasn't exactly comfortable to kneel on, but no way was he making any sudden moves.

Deryn's gaze went past him. "And Eve too?" he checked. "Tristan?"

Abel was silent. It was obvious, wasn't it? But he couldn't say it, not when...

The human, who couldn't hear his heart beating too hard or smell his fear, somehow reacted all the same. His hand on Abel's hair stopped but stayed, and he bent forward, only stilling when Abel looked up and met his eyes. "I'm not... I *promised*, I won't tell anyone. I just— I'm trying to—" He stopped. "Why are you telling me this? Isn't it dangerous or...?"

"Illegal," Abel offered. "By pack law."

"Oh." Deryn's hand fell away, but a moment later he made up for it by taking hold of Abel's elbow and pushing him up. "Get up, that can't be comfortable, and—" He stuttered a little when Abel made it to verticality, perhaps remembering he was naked, but he simply tilted his head to the side and continued, "Maybe get dressed."

DERYN

A mong the very weird things he'd learned about the world, this was without a doubt at the very top. On the other hand, if he ranked those things according to how much he wanted them to be true, then this was undoubtedly at the very top too. In a world with rapidly rising sea levels, with people who murdered each other for rocks and didn't care if others starved while they threw out enough food to drown in, there were apparently also undercover werewolves.

Among a million other things too upsetting for anyone to think about if they wanted to do anything but curl up in a ball and cry... This was beautiful, elegant, *magical*.

Deryn didn't believe in magic, except, of course, Deryn believed in evidence.

And he believed in Abel, he realised when the other man walked back in dressed in comfortable clothes. The suit was still folded over the back of his chair; both forgotten and a very expensive and incongruous reminder of what had happened.

Abel, who was not only beautiful and thoughtful and funny, but also, apparently, sometimes howled at the moon.

"You're still here," he said.

"You're still a werewolf," Deryn replied, eyeing the folded clothes meaningfully, but his eyes were drawn to the man who'd worn them almost at once. "Are there mermaids?" He couldn't have said how his brain jumped there, but maybe it was too many surprises in too short a time because it came right out of his mouth.

"What?" There was some satisfaction in Abel's confusion, he could admit.

"No offence," Deryn added. "But if there are werewolves, there should be mermaids."

"Err... I don't know. Why?"

"And vampires, but I don't fancy meeting any," Deryn clarified. "I mean, just, let's say there's magic or the supernatural or whatever, then it would make no sense for only part of it to be true."

Abel tilted his head, laughing a little hysterically. Deryn was tempted himself. "Why? Just because science discovers things that are true, it doesn't follow that everything science theorizes is true, does it?"

"I guess that's true, but I still vote for mermaids," Deryn insisted. He exhaled and stretched his hand towards Abel, palm up. It was absurd to be nervous, of course, the guy had literally come out as a magical creature for him.

Abel pulled him to his feet easily. Deryn wasn't sure if he was supernaturally strong or just... "I'll see if I can find you any," Abel offered.

Deryn clutched at his hand, looking down and swallowing. "I mean, I guess... it's not a big deal." He laughed because hell, it was a *relief* to be the one with a secret that didn't matter for once. At least he was pretty sure... "I'm trans," he spit out.

"Oh, I thought so," Abel said, and Deryn tried to step back and found Abel's other arm around his back. He tensed, confused. "Sticker!" Abel added, too quick, and also nonsensically enough to make Deryn look up at him. The guy was so tall he had to tilt his head sideways to manage but it was worth it. "You have a sticker in your diary? Pink and light blue?"

"Oh," he said. "I could just be... an ally."

"Thing is..." Abel sighed and his hands loosened on Deryn, which was *not* what Deryn wanted. If Abel didn't think... If Abel knew and wanted to hold on, then he should. But Abel didn't let go, just kept his left hand against Deryn's waist, a suggestion of closeness. Deryn was still holding the other one—big but almost hairless—in his own. "Even when I'm human, I can... well, I can tell things, hear them and..." Deryn glanced up right in time to see his Adam's apple bobbing as he swallowed. "And smell them."

"So you can just tell," he said and it came out flat. He'd worked harder at this than he'd ever done at sculpture, and of course Abel had seen right through it.

"Hey," Abel tugged a little at his hand. "I didn't know at first. I don't think Eve knows," he added quickly. "But it's *you*. You must have seen me looking, right? That's how I saw the sticker too, I just... I couldn't look away." His hands were too still, like he was forcing himself not to move.

He hadn't seemed even half as nervous when he'd been a huge white wolf.

Abel's fingers twitched but he didn't try to stop Deryn when he took a step back. He'd forgotten all about the chair he'd been sitting in minutes before so when he crashed right into it, it almost toppled and sent him down too. In a blink, Abel was back on his knees, hands on either side of the seat, elbows locked to keep Deryn in place. Deryn blinked at him from his seat. He hadn't really had time to feel afraid. "Is this a werewolf thing too?"

"What?"

"The furniture attacks."

Abel snorted, shaking his head. He didn't get up, just waited, and it was impossible to see him right there and not remember that less than half an hour earlier he'd been *a wolf.*

Deryn wanted to touch his hair, a little tangled, and see if it was as soft now as it'd been on the wolf. And ten minutes earlier, when Abel had knelt at his feet like some sort of supplicant knight... Naked.

He shook his head, snorting. Here he was, with a beautiful man declaring his devotion, and he was worrying about whether he could pass among werewolves. "And you don't... care?"

"Care?" Abel repeated, he was frowning, which Deryn could only tell because he was so close since his eyebrows were blond enough to be hard to see. Maybe Abel was just stuck being cheerful by a lack of any visible means to frown. Deryn found his hand on Abel's jaw, his thumb trying to smooth out the thin hairs of his eyebrow.

"You don't care what I... what I look like?"

"I *like* what you look like," Abel assured him, tentatively putting his hands atop Deryn's knees. "And I was hoping to see more, like, not right now—"

His lips were still moving when Deryn drew him into the kiss, but he melted at once, letting out a sound very much like a whimper as Deryn sucked on his tongue, lapping at his mouth, *finally*. He tasted like tea, his mouth hot and slick, his fingers digging into Deryn's thighs a little too hard like he'd forgotten to be careful.

Abel was considerably larger than him, which came in handy when Deryn leaned forward a little too much and they overbalanced, crashing to the floor. Even with Abel acting as a cushion, Deryn paused, but his lover seemed to have missed their fall altogether, too busy planting a trail of kisses along the line of Deryn's jaw that left him trembling.

When he rolled them over and it was Deryn's turn to lie on the floor, he pulled back, twisting out of a kiss like he was ripping off a limb. "Abel!" he panted.

The other man froze, pulling back to meet his eyes.

"Bed?" Deryn suggested, even as his fingers traced Abel's lips.

Abel scrunched his eyes shut, shuddering against him, and Deryn's hips shoved up, not caring much about discomfort when—

The next seconds became a blur when Abel used his speed to what Deryn's brain eventually deciphered was rolling onto his own back with Deryn in his arms, then jumping to his feet and standing. By the time they reacquired verticality, Deryn's nails were digging into the exposed skin of his neck and his legs had found their way around Abel's waist, the pressure against his groin enough to make his vision double even without the werewolf antics.

"Um, okay?" Abel checked.

And Deryn's laughter was a little manic, sure, but who could blame him? He muffled it against Abel's mouth, kissing him hard enough to make it clear he could speed up again any time.

Somehow, they got to the bedroom. There were candles there, but Deryn only cared because he almost kicked one. Abel deposited him in the bed like he was made of porcelain—or paper—and Deryn sighed against the soft duvet, toeing off his dress shoes and moaning quietly. He must have closed his eyes because when he looked at Abel, he was naked again. Just standing there at the foot of the bed in all his glory, skin evenly tanned all over, hair growing darker as it travelled down his chest to his groin as if to lead the eyes to the crowning glory of his cock.

Deryn's mouth watered a little, even as his brain couldn't help but catalogue.

"Deryn?" Abel asked softly and he looked up, cheeks heating up. "Can I see you?"

He swallowed. It was... It was fine, obviously. Abel *knew*, he reminded himself. Maybe not the specifics but... He nodded and pushed himself up into a sitting position, dragging his shirt over his head, not allowing himself the hesitation.

Abel sighed, taking a step closer to the bed and placing the tips of his fingers on Deryn's left bicep. "Lifting a lot of desks, are we?" he teased, cupping the muscle. His hand was hot and a little callused, but so careful. Deryn shivered, tilting his head back to watch the emotions flickering across Abel's face.

Abel's knee landed on the bed between the V of his own legs and he leaned forward and placed a careful kiss on the tip of Deryn's collarbone, setting him shivering. *Faster*, he wanted to say. *Just do it*. But as Abel's kisses travelled down his chest, his other hand squeezing his thigh close enough to Deryn's cock to make the distance painful, he found himself relaxing instead.

Abel nuzzled at Deryn's jaw, somehow managing to drag his nose against the line of his jugular so gently Deryn's brain seemed to stutter and his whole body arched, seeking more. He was on his back, he realised, and he wasn't sure when he'd got there. Not that he cared, not when Abel was above him; one hand tickling at his belly as he ran his nails right along the boundary of his trousers, a thumb circling his nipple, the heavy solid heat of his naked thighs pressed against the outside of Deryn's clothed legs.

"Can I?" he whispered, pressing the button of his dress trousers against the skin of his belly in a tease that had his dick twitching. Deryn moaned, suddenly remembering his hands were free and lifting one to tug at Abel's elbow.

The message was received, but Abel ignored his urgency, popping the button and rubbing at the skin underneath as if it needed soothing. Deryn moaned as the sensation shot down, making his hips arch to try and get... Abel exhaled, hot and wet, and took his mouth again, a liquid kiss building force like a tsunami until he was lying on top of Deryn, chests rubbing together and Abel's arse pressing down on his knees where he sat atop him, but nothing where Deryn needed it most. Damn the height difference!

"Abel," he whispered, hoarse and so openly needy he'd have blushed if his face hadn't been as flushed as it could possibly get.

"Oh, yeah," Abel responded, sounding equally breathless.

Deryn bit his lip not to complain as his mouth was abandoned as his lover crawled downwards. It was worth it for the zip being pulled down, letting in the air and making him clench as Abel let out a hungry sound.

He was not ready for the pressure of a kiss against his cock, not even through the cotton, and he whimpered, hips jumping up.

Abel groaned. "Oh, goddess, you smell..." If he meant to say more, Deryn missed it when he pressed a harder kiss to his erection, getting his tongue involved and wetting his boxers.

It was enough teasing he was unsurprised to realise his right hand was clutching at Abel's hair to keep him in place. Not that Abel seemed to need to breathe, alternating between lapping and sucking, his hands cupping Deryn's arse and encouraging him to thrust.

He didn't ask permission to tug down his shorts and from one moment to the next, his mouth was *on Deryn's cock*. He arched, screaming as his body sparkled, cock jumping, clenching hard against the emptiness.

When his brain was once again able to tell his toes apart from his nose, he felt Abel panting against his hip, body held tightly controlled above him.

Deryn tugged on his hair. "Condom?" His voice was a mess, but he couldn't stop smiling.

Abel almost fell off the bed to get to his bedside table. Ears still ringing, Deryn turned his head to watch him, kicking his underwear and pants off. There were a handful of candles about the place in little glass lamps. Had Abel set them up when he'd gone to get dressed?

He forgot to wonder when Abel turned around and did his trick of fast-forwarding his hands until the condom seemed to be straining a little around his massive erection.

Deryn couldn't *wait* to have him inside.

The bottle of lube startled him a little because half of him had wanted... But of course that wasn't what Abel had signed up for.

"Deryn?" His lover had paused, kneeling over him once more, his hard cock in sharp contrast with his soft expression. "You okay?"

He offered a shaky nod. "Yeah, I can turn around."

"Please don't." Abel bit his lip. "I mean, I know I'm..." He waved down at himself. "Are you worried? We don't have to—"

"I'm not," Deryn cut in. "I can take you, big wolf," he added. He wished Abel had prepared the condom instead of the candles, just so they didn't have to talk so much. Abel had been doing just fine without talking and whatever he did would be wonderful, Deryn just knew it, so—

"Do you want to take me?" Abel asked, completely serious. "Because there's other things we can do if—"

"No," Deryn said at once, reaching out and tugging at his forearm. Abel went with it, crawling closer and Deryn stretched his neck until he could reunite their mouths. Kissing was easy, no words needed and no words possible beyond a few gasped syllables. And their bodies followed along, Abel aligning their hips and bending himself in half to lick into his mouth. His cock was a line of heat brushing all too gently along Deryn's side. "Abel," he begged. "Please, just..."

Abel's hand left his waist and travelled down his stomach until he found Deryn's cock, petting it for just long enough to get it hardening again. "Deryn?" he said, and Deryn looked up to find his lover's eyes just as Abels's fingers skimmed lower and found his opening. He clenched, slick and hot and so... Abel was still watching him when his eyes fluttered open, and he didn't look away as the tips dipped into the heat of Deryn's front hole.

"Oh," Deryn exhaled, clenching. "Abel..."

"Good?" his lover checked, giving him a little more and then taking it back.

Deryn dug his nails into his forearm and shoved his hips up. "Yes!"

Abel's fingers might not have been as thick as other parts of his person, but having two of them inside was definitely a very good start. "Goddess, you're so wet..." he murmured. And that was weird, Deryn thought, or it should have been, but Abel's fingers were curling just right, like he—

Deryn whimpered, and pulled until Abel took his fingers out. "Just— Just *fuck me*, I can't— *Do it*," he demanded, glancing up.

Abel's lips were parted and his normally tanned skin was flushed dark. He nodded, looking dazed.

Deryn half rolled and got the lubricant, then squeezed it over his own groin. He was wet but even so, Abel was big and he couldn't wait a second longer.

He gasped a little at the cold liquid over his cock, but it helped a little with how close he was to coming again, and it made it easy to take a handful, rub it a little between his palms and grab hold of Abel's gorgeous erection, coating it with enough lube to get it through a solid wall.

Abel startled in his hold, but didn't object.

"I'm ready," Deryn told him, letting go and putting a hand between his own legs, right where Abel's fingers had been. His heart was about to explode, but it was just... He had to at least *ask*.

Abel's eyes flickered down. "Slow," he warned, but that was all the hesitation he showed before putting his hands under Deryn's knees and spreading him open a little further. Deryn relaxed onto his back, trusting his body to his lover, and he felt Abel's cock head bump his own, then get closer to where he ached. Even just the head seemed too much, but as he inhaled, his body welcomed it, letting Abel in.

"Deryn," Abel's whisper was half pained plea, half prayer. "Oh, goddess, Deryn, you—" He sank another inch, big enough Deryn's body resisted. Abel paused, allowing him the time, and then gently pushed a little more. And Deryn let him do it, allowed himself to be touched, inside and out. Abel's hands were running up and down his thighs like he'd need to sculpt them later, his mouth peppering kisses down Deryn's chest once he was close enough to reach—nuzzling at nipples and scars with equal fervour—and his voice, soft but steady, promise after endearment after gratitude that felt misplaced when Deryn felt like he was being lit up from the inside.

Impossibly, it started to feel better once the slicked length of his lover was not just fully inside him but also able to retreat and thrust in again. Deryn hooked his knees around his back and held on for the ride, half forgetting about his cock until Abel said his name and reached for it, squeezing with a hand that was wet enough to short-circuit Deryn's body.

He screamed, body contracting around Abel's cock as he came, feeling Abel's cock inside him respond, seeming to grow even as Deryn's body shrank.

Abel groaned in his ear, lips clumsy, teeth grazing his neck before he sharply turned his mouth away.

Separating seemed almost sacrilegious, but the condom had to be disposed of, and his body probably needed a little rest, too. Abel, who was apparently a supernatural creature immune to such prosaic problems as lower temperatures, flopped onto his back, panting like he'd run a marathon.

Deryn let his eyes close, a little cold but not enough to move, and then Abel's weight disappeared and he was tugged closer and rolled away, the duvet coming loose and landing on top of them.

He laughed, perhaps a little too high. And he didn't *care*. It didn't matter. Not with Abel's arm around his waist, big body doing more to keep him warm than the blanket.

"**Y**ou have done that before," he said softly against Abel's chest. There might have been some sleep at some point and his stomach was making it known it would not stand for the lack of sustenance long. But he didn't want to venture outside the nest of blankets just then.

"Mmm?"

"The... The fingering."

"Oh, with... that equipment?" Abel said tentatively, Deryn could hear his heart racing under his ear.

He rubbed his side reassuringly, it was his body and maybe he hadn't chosen the factory settings, but he was happy with the current setup—especially if his new lover was that good at turning his gears. "Yeah."

"Yeah," Abel agreed, leaning back a little and blinking his pretty eyes at Deryn. "Did practice make perfect?"

And he really deserved the pillow to the head just for that.

ABEL

"Were you sure I would be cool about...?" Deryn asked, waving a hand.

"Pretty sure."

"Sure enough to light the candles?" Deryn teased.

Abel laughed, shrugging and then curling up closer. "I get a little sappy," he conceded with as much dignity as he could manage. "But I'm sure the man who organized a whole week of St. Valentine's celebrations won't be casting any stones."

He laughed, finding a pillow to hit him with. "Oh my god, are you never gonna let that go?"

Abel shoved the pillow back and rolled on top of him. "Nah, but feel free to distract me."

A kiss was, in all truth, a win for everyone.

Epilogue

"**I** can't believe you're doing this to me," Eve groaned, covering her face.

"A home-made dinner?" Abel asked her innocently.

He got a glare in return and he squinted... *Was she wearing eye shadow?* "Getting all sappy!" she told him with an eye roll.

"What's sappy?" asked Tristan coming into the kitchen. He inhaled and offered Abel a brilliant smile.

"You two!" their daughter told them resignedly. She waited until Abel was offering Tristan a spoonful of lentils to add, "Maybe *I* will get a boyfriend too."

The lentils ended half on the floor, half on Abel's apron, and when he glanced up he saw for the first time since that night, Tristan looking lost.

Abel rolled his eyes at him, then turned to Eve. "Sure, go ahead. You can bring him to dinner with all of us," he offered with a brilliant smile.

His daughter was plenty smart enough to realise what any teenage boy would feel in the presence of four adult male authority figures. Her alarmed expression looked remarkably like Tristan's. Of course, she was his kid too. "Maybe I will get a *girlfriend*," she shot back.

Abel shrugged and gestured welcomingly. "If you can find the right person at your age," he told her, relaxing as the words came. "Then you are way ahead of us."

[The End]

This novella belongs in the same universe as "Runt of the Litter"[1], Tristan and Lyall's romance.

Runt of the Litter

A young insecure alpha, an older omega determined to keep his freedom, and the injustice neither of them can permit to go on.

Lyall is failing at alphahood like a pro—he's presented, but he's still too skinny and too short, and nowhere near aggressive enough to put off his packmates' constant reminders that he looks a lot like an omega. They have him convinced he'll never be worth anything.

Tristan doesn't want an alpha: he wants to give other omegas a chance at the freedom he's carved out for himself. He's figured out enough loopholes to keep himself unbonded and free to do it, but he's still only one person and there are a lot of people who need to hear what he is teaching. When he meets Lyall, he realises the young alpha would make an ideal assistant.

Their meeting is brief, but their connection is undeniable and as they work together with an ocean between them, it gets harder to deny their own lives have been changed forever....

A coming of age romance between a young alpha and the older omega who teaches him to believe in himself and learns to believe in them both in the process.

Lyall

'Runt of the litter' was actually one of the nicest things he got called by his siblings. Sometimes they'd even say it fondly instead of mockingly, though Lyall didn't appreciate it either way.

His dad had made it clear early on it was not acceptable to make fun of him for being small, so they didn't dare do it at all in front of their parents and older siblings.

They were all grown now and it didn't even happen that often anymore. When it did, it was more leftover habit than actual aggression—the kind of sibling rivalry that could have meant they trusted each other enough to be rude. But it *didn't*. It was just true, and it was like a sore place inside him, the knowledge they thought that of him.

They were his littermates, not twins but almost as good. They'd shared everything from the moment they'd come to be, and they had been meant to share everything from then on.

They did, the four of them.

But Lyall was too weird, too small, too weak.

In turn, his older siblings had always been kinder to him than to the rest of his litter, but in a way that overcompensation had set him apart for his weakness just as much as his agemates' disdain.

And for all his dad defended him, he *had* chosen to start trying the new experimental birth control methods right after the five of them had been born.

Not that Lyall blamed him—he'd been teased enough about how he'd obviously be an omega that he was better informed than most about the hardships of pregnancy.

Omeganess was the one thing his siblings wouldn't make fun of—but other pack kids, who'd bought on the stupid human ideas that a man being anything like a woman was embarrassing, said it often enough that he'd ended up believing it would happen.

He respected his dad and he wouldn't have minded being an omega so much—it wasn't like anyone would look at him twice without pheromones intervening.

Lyall would have liked being more attractive, instead of just small. At 5'7 he barely made it to average for human standards, among wolves who regularly reached 6 feet as teenagers, he often felt like a child.

He was ready to be a beta forever—most people were—and to become an omega.

It should have come as no surprise when he presented alpha instead—after all, Nature had made it clear it liked screwing him over from the moment he'd been born.

Tristan

Tristan dropped his bag on the cheap hotel carpet, nose wrinkling at the lingering scents of disinfectant, sweat and cigarettes. A decade had passed since smoking had been prohibited in most public places, but of course the little addicts kept sneaking around polluting everyone's air.

He could have stayed with the Williamson Pack, their alpha had offered him a room to himself at his home.

But he didn't like being indebted to any of his clients. He was well-aware his message often wasn't well-received. A lot of people—especially alphas—didn't see why omegas couldn't keep popping out as many pups as they would, like they had for millennia.

Never mind how uncomfortable pregnancy was or how little time that left to look after said children, or how child mortality was extremely rare now that humans no longer believed in them and nature had been trampled into submission.

Never mind that some omegas might want a life beyond making a home for an alpha and children.

The alphas often agreed to receive Tristan and let him speak, probably figuring he would just tell omegas that fucking their alphas a lot *before* heat would make the full moon easier on them and multiples less likely.

But Tristan had a lot more to offer than some of them wanted their omegas to hear—and he himself was proof that biology didn't have to rule your life.

He exhaled and got his tablet out, checking the charge, the projector went next. He was here to offer people choices, not rant. And hopefully... well, choices were the reason he was here.

He missed his pack, especially Eve. But they knew he needed to do this and it was only a few times a year that he was gone this long—there just happened to be several large packs surrounding the almost untouched land along Warri Parri River.

The Williamson Pack was traditional enough to keep a hall for pack meetings, but it was nothing like the restored medieval building Tristan's own pack used back in Wales. The ancient civilizations who'd inhabited this place hadn't had need of sturdy buildings to protect them from the weather, instead they'd learned to navigate with the wind and to supplement their diet by taking advantage of the flow of the river.

This building was a pleasantly uniform red brick and blue windows combination, likely dating from the same period as the rows of two story-houses right behind it.

Inside, someone was setting up basic foldable Ikea chairs—this pack was well-off but not affluent. They had made an effort to alternate black and white ones to create and interesting effect. Tristan noticed the hangings on the brick walls, untreated brick too, followed the same colour scheme.

The enterprising decorator seemed to become aware of his presence just then. Tristan opened his mouth to shout a greeting when a whiff of the other werewolf's scent reached him and the words dried in his mouth.

He was alone with an alpha.

He shoved the thought away, furious with himself, and raised a hand to wave at the stranger preparing the stage for him.

The boy stopped half a room away—as far as alphas went, he was far from intimidating. Shorter than Tristan and kinda skinny like he still wasn't quite done growing, which was interesting because alphas had an upsurge in testosterone when they presented that made them bulk up almost without trying. But maybe he was one of those rare cases that presented very early...

"Doctor Sanders?" His voice was smooth like silk and lower than he'd have expected from someone who looked so young. Young, but not a boy, that was clear by his manner and the respectful nod he offered, hands going into his jean pockets—well away from Tristan himself. This alpha knew he'd startled him, which made Tristan want to step up to him and his wolf cringe, and he was trying to put him at ease.

"Yes," he managed. "I like to be early." He glanced around, pretending his pulse hadn't picked up. "Thank you for all this, it looks great."

Lyall

L yall knew he was staring—it was rude as fuck and, coming from a strange alpha, also kind of creepy. It was just... he'd read Doctor Tristan Sanders's leaflets on family planning and reproductive control for omegas. There were only a few people in the world bothering to research the topic and in the middle of rural Australia, Lyall hadn't expected to have the chance to meet any of them.

Keep reading...[1]

Other Books by N.J. Lysk

My site[1] – Complete book list[2] – Free Reads[3] – Mailing list [4] – Payhip Store[5]

[6]

The Stars of the Pack:[7]

1. **Omega for the Pack[8] (Available in audio[9])** – When Ray presents as an omega instead of an alpha, his life changes forever. As a male omega, he's expected to mate with a select group of alphas and start a pack of his own. **A/B/O, M/M/M/M/M/M, M/M, mpreg,**

1. https://readerlinks.com/l/3217648

2. https://readerlinks.com/l/1729103

3. https://readerlinks.com/l/3217652

4. https://readerlinks.com/l/3218944

5. https://readerlinks.com/l/3218943

6.   https://readerlinks.com/l/3217648

7. https://readerlinks.com/l/1332357

8. https://readerlinks.com/l/1332298

9. https://readerlinks.com/l/3900407

dubcon. *Also in German, French, Italian & Portuguese.*

1. **Simpler than Most**[10] *(an interlude)* – Sergi has stopped lying to himself: he's had a crush on a guy for a while. But it turns out telling yourself the truth is just the first step of a long journey. *Also in Spanish, German, Italian & French bilingual editions.*

2. **Alpha for the Pack**[11] – Ray wasn't ready to become an omega, but he's come to accept his fate... until it seems the pack might need even more of him than he can give.

3. **Protectors of the Pack**[12] – Alec and Gabriel are Ray's alphas first and foremost and nothing to each other. But three years ago... things were very different. Get the free short prequel[13] here!

4. **Beloved of the Pack**[14] – An omega is essential to his pack. But an omega is just a man. And a man needs to be loved. *Can you share your body and not share your heart?*

5. **Betas Aside**[15] – Marisa never hesitated to go to her brother's aid—even when he has what she wants most in the world and can never have. But maybe where there's love, there is a way.

---

10. https://readerlinks.com/l/1332338

11. https://readerlinks.com/l/1332306

12. https://readerlinks.com/l/1332309

13. https://readerlinks.com/l/935814

14. https://readerlinks.com/l/1332316

15. https://readerlinks.com/l/1332327

5.1) **Around the Hearth**[16] – When Marisa suggests cutting a tree for Christmas, Ray's reaction shocks everyone. But there is something much deeper at play than pregnancy hormones and Josh is prepared to help Ray get to the bottom of it all.

O r get the complete series with all extras here[17].

1. **Runt of the Litter**[18] – An older omega who is ready to change the world, a young alpha who doesn't believe in his own potential; a love that's stronger than distance, age or inclination. **A/B/O. M/M. Age gap. Long-distance.**

2. **Paper Kisses**[19] (**Available in audio**[20]) – Abel's not the kind of alpha to make a fuss when his omega ex gets together with someone else, but he's still lonely enough to seek out their kid's teacher to complain about wasting time to celebrate Valentine's day. He doesn't expect to find a lot more than paper hearts. **M/M. Age gap. Human/werewolf. Sweet.**

Rules to Break:

- **Not Destiny**[21] – Thomas and Uriel were never meant

---

16. https://readerlinks.com/l/3497534

17. https://readerlinks.com/l/1332357

18. https://readerlinks.com/l/1332330

19. https://readerlinks.com/l/1332367

20. https://readerlinks.com/l/3900407

to be together. If they choose each other anyway, can they beat the odds? **An Alpha/Beta romance.**

- **Cracking Ice**[22] series (7 episodes) – Hockey means everything to them both... Until they meet each other. **An Alpha/Omega hockey romance.**
- A Unique Perspective[23] – Yadriel doesn't look like an omega, but to the eyes of a very interested beta photographer, maybe there is a lot more to him than his size. **A beta/omega BDSM romance.**

Deep in the Dark – (Erotica by N.Y. Lysk):[24]

- **The Weight of Duty**[25] – Now that the twins are of age, their uncle takes them in hand to teach them their marital duties. But the experience will be very different for each of them. **Dub-con, feminization, medical body modification, abuse, group sex, arranged marriage, betrayal, incest.**
- **Soldier On**[26] – When a humble young man is captured by the enemy lord during battle, he is expected to offer defeat to his captor by allowing him to bed him. But he is young enough that the act might unintentionally activate a hormonal process that will irreversibly feminise him. **Dub-con, Non-con,**

21. https://readerlinks.com/l/1332321

22. https://readerlinks.com/l/1332310

23. https://readerlinks.com/l/1430496

24. https://readerlinks.com/l/956756

25. https://readerlinks.com/l/1586203

26. https://readerlinks.com/l/1332324

mpreg, feminization, debasement.

- **The Will of Heaven**[27] – Prince Hiram of Pradeira is deemed unfit to be king after his father dies. But as a direct descendant of the gods, only those of his bloodline can reign and so to avoid civil war, he agrees to have a child with each of the princes of the other noble houses of the kingdom so that his first born and heir can inherit the throne from whoever fathered him. **Dub-con, mpreg, feminization, medical kink, debasement.** *Also in German & Italian.*

- **His Brother's Dowry**[28] – Tony agrees to accompany his brother to a new pack, knowing he will have to submit to alphas in the absence of omegas but willing to sacrifice his comfort to give Peter a chance to find love. But his brother is already in love with an omega girl and he will give anything to get her. Even Tony. **Dub-con, non-con, mpreg, feminization, debasement, body modification.**

- **The Alpha Solution**[29] – Junen will be the next alpha of his pack... until one day he's taken by a stranger—an alpha his father rejected and who's determined to use Junen to get to him. By making him his omega. **Non-con, mpreg, kidnapping, feminization, fisting, debasement, body modification, group sex, abuse.**

- **More forbidden shorts found only on my website.**[30]

---

27. https://readerlinks.com/l/1332326

28. https://readerlinks.com/l/1332355

29. https://readerlinks.com/l/1332320

30. https://readerlinks.com/l/956756

<u>Standalones</u>:

- **A Light in Winter**[31] (**Available in audio**[32]) – Alone and trapped by a dangerous arctic storm, two young men have no choice but to confront their feelings for each other. **A/B/O. Cousins. Werewolves. Isolation.**

- **The Omega Sacrifice**[33] - *Fate deals the cards, but you can still play your hand.* When a young omega is sent away to marry a strange alpha, he has no choice but to face who he is. **An arranged marriage omegaverse romance.**

- **A Bond Unbroken**[34] – When Lia presents as an omega, her best friend offers her anything she needs. But Lia's been in love with Amira for years and whatever her wolf wants, her heart cannot take what's not freely given. **Best friends to lovers. F/F. A/B/O.** *Also in Spanish, German, Italian & French.*

- **Truth Unveiled:**[35] When Kala comes out at work to spite her biphobic coworker, she ends up in need of a fake date for the Christmas party. Her best friend immediately offers to help, but for how long can they handle the pretence? **F/F. Shifters, not A/B/O. A best friends fake dating novella.**

- **Omega Under The Moon**[36] (**Available in audio**[37]) –

---

31. https://readerlinks.com/l/1586233

32. https://readerlinks.com/l/3900407

33. https://readerlinks.com/l/1430436

34. https://readerlinks.com/l/1332433

35. https://readerlinks.com/l/2383454

School is over and Cole is ready to take a break before adult life starts, but when a camping trip with his two best mates turns into something much wilder, it'll change his life forever. **A/B/O. M/M/M.** *Also in French, German & Italian.*

- **Omega Under the Moon: six months later[38]** – It's been six months since Cole presented omega and ended up dating his two alpha best friends. Time has run out and certain needs must be met. But is their bond strong enough to survive heat and all the changes it will bring? **Mpreg.**

- **Omega On A Mission[39]** - omegas are carers, not fighters, and Gabi is happy looking after his alpha. But when he comes across an animal in danger, his protective instincts flare up, and nobody wants to get in the way of an omega on a mission. **A/B/O.**

Intertwined Fates:[40]

- **Not to be Borne[41]** – When his twin brother presents as an omega, Michuá feels like the world is ending. In a way, becoming an omega himself seems like the only way to stay together... But Zybyn's new alpha wants a lot more than they have bargained for and in a journey

36. https://readerlinks.com/l/1332329

37. https://readerlinks.com/l/3900407

38. https://readerlinks.com/l/3914687

39. https://readerlinks.com/l/1332322

40. https://readerlinks.com/l/3427158

41. https://readerlinks.com/l/1332478

towards a strange land, there is nothing to stop him from taking it. **Non-con, abuse, twincest, HEA.**

- **Always[42] His** – When Shane unexpectedly presents as an omega during the full moon, his twin brother steps in to protect him from the alphas who'd claim him... But Tim is also an alpha. **A/B/O. M/M. Twincest. Also in French & German.**

- **Always Mine[43]** – Imagine there's only one person in the world you can't have... And he's your soulmate. **A/B/O. M/M. Twincest. Tim's story.**

- **The Realm of the Impossible[44]** – The Queen is dead and Lorax is ready to take his rightful place when an intimate betrayal leaves him with no choice but to surrender his throne or lose his only remaining family. At this unbearable crossroad, Lorax can watch the new Queen lead his country to a war that will destroy it, or indulge his enemy's sole weakness: himself. **A Taboo M/M Royal Romance.**

- **Entwined: a l[45]ove story** – The Thorne triplets are nearly ready to leave for university, but they can't imagine life without each other. Until a kiss becomes a betrayal none of them know how to repair.

Werewolves of Windermere:

1. **The Mating Habits of Werewolves[46]** – Devlin is an

42. https://readerlinks.com/l/1332301

43. https://readerlinks.com/l/3427160

44. https://readerlinks.com/l/1332328

45. https://readerlinks.com/l/3900436

omega with ambitions that have nothing to do with alphas, but when destiny comes calling, he may not have that much of a choice. **A/B/O, M/M/M, mpreg.**

2. **Alphas Alone**[47] – An alpha werewolf has some responsibilities he can't ignore: finding an omega, protecting his pack, not falling for another alpha.

3. **The Parenting Habits of Werewolves**[48] – With children in common, Devlin, Naveen and Rami know their fates are bound together, but can they find a balance beyond domesticity? And can they build a love that can last? **The conclusion to the M/M/M Mpreg Romance.**

---

46. https://readerlinks.com/l/1332319

47. https://readerlinks.com/l/1332341

48. https://readerlinks.com/l/1430466

About the author

N.J. Lysk (pronouns: whatever) is a queer one—in almost every sense of the word—for whom stories have always been their one true home. She studied linguistics and literature (which is to say, someone offered him a genuine excuse to read professionally) and ended up teaching, but writing is their one true love.

Addicted to angst, enamoured of mpreg and always ready to try a new kink (in a book, that's it!) she became hooked into the omegaverse through fanfic (but he doesn't have the patience to write other people's characters) and has recently expanded from werewolves to hockey players.

If your heart veers towards the dark, look for the **N.Y. Lysk** instead & subscribe to the Dark & Taboo list[1] (these books all come with serious warnings!).

Join their mailing list[2] for book updates and free books, updates and more cool things.

Books can be acquired directly from the website at a reduced rate—new releases also become available there earlier.

---

1.   https://readerlinks.com/l/3218963
2.   https://readerlinks.com/l/3218944